ALSO BY STEPHEN KING

STEPHEN KING

THE SUN DOG

SCRIBNER

New York London Toronto Sydney New Delhi

Scribner
An Imprint of Simon & Schuster, Inc.
1230 Avenue of the Americas
New York, NY 10020

This Scribner trade paperback edition December 2018

For information about special discounts for bulk purchases, please contact Simon & Schuster Special Sales at 1-866-506-1949 or business@simonandschuster.com.

The Simon & Schuster Speakers Bureau can bring authors to your live event. For more information or to book an event, contact the Simon & Schuster Speakers Bureau at 1-866-248-3049 or visit our website at www.simonspeakers.com.

Manufactured in the United States of America

3 5 7 9 10 8 6 4

Library of Congress Cataloging-in-Publication Data is available.

ISBN 978-1-9821-1542-5
ISBN 978-1-9821-1543-2 (ebook)

THIS IS IN MEMORY OF JOHN D. MACDONALD.
I MISS YOU, OLD FRIEND—AND YOU WERE RIGHT
ABOUT THE TIGERS.

A NOTE ON THE SUN DOG

Every now and then someone will ask me, "When are you going to get tired of this horror stuff, Steve, and write something serious?"

I used to believe the implied insult in this question was accidental, but as the years go by I have become more and more convinced that it is not. I watch the faces of the people who drop that particular dime, you see, and most of them look like bombardiers waiting to see if their last stick of bombs is going to fall wide or hit the targeted factory or munitions dump dead on.

The fact is, almost all of the stuff I have written—and that includes a lot of the funny stuff—was written in a serious frame of mind. I can remember very few occasions when I sat at the typewriter laughing uncontrollably over some wild and crazy bit of fluff I had just finished churning out. I'm never going to be Reynolds Price or Larry Woiwode—it isn't in me—but that doesn't mean I don't care as deeply about what I do. I have to do what I *can* do, however—as Nils Lofgren once put it, "I gotta be my dirty self . . . I won't play no jive."

If *real*—meaning!! SOMETHING THAT COULD ACTUALLY HAPPEN!!—is your definition of serious, you are in the wrong place and you should by all means leave the building. But please remember as you go that I'm not the only one doing business at this particular site; Franz Kafka had an office here, and George Orwell, and Shirley Jackson, and Jorge Luis Borges, and Jonathan Swift, and Lewis Carroll. A glance at the directory in the lobby shows the present tenants include Thomas Berger, Ray Bradbury, Jonathan Carroll, Thomas

Pynchon, Thomas Disch, Kurt Vonnegut, Jr., Peter Straub, Joyce Carol Oates, Isaac Bashevis Singer, Katherine Dunn, and Mark Halpern.

I am doing what I do for the most serious reasons: love, money, and obsession. The tale of the irrational is the sanest way I know of expressing the world in which I live. These tales have served me as instruments of both metaphor and morality; they continue to offer the best window I know on the question of how we perceive things and the corollary question of how we do or do not behave on the basis of our perceptions. I have explored these questions as well as I can within the limits of my talent and intelligence. I am no one's National Book Award or Pulitzer Prize winner, but I'm serious, all right. If you don't believe anything else, believe this: when I take you by your hand and begin to talk, my friend, I believe every word I say.

A lot of the things I have to say—those Really Serious Things—have to do with the small-town world in which I was raised and where I still live. Stories and novels are scale models of what we laughingly call "real life," and I believe that lives as they are lived in small towns are scale models of what we laughingly call "society." This idea is certainly open to argument, and argument is perfectly fine (without it, a lot of literature teachers and critics would be looking for work); I'm just saying that a writer needs some sort of launching pad, and aside from the firm belief that a story may exist with honor for its own self, the idea of the small town as social and psychological microcosm is mine. I began experimenting with this sort of thing in *Carrie*, and continued on a more ambitious level with *'Salem's Lot*. I never really hit my stride, however, until *The Dead Zone*.

That was, I think, the first of my Castle Rock stories (and Castle Rock is really just the town of Jerusalem's Lot without the vampires). In the years since it was written, Castle Rock has increasingly become "my town," in the sense that the mythical city of Isola is Ed McBain's town and the West Virginia village of Glory was Davis Grubb's town. I have been called back there time and time again to examine the lives of its residents and the geographies which seem to rule their lives—Castle Hill and Castle View, Castle Lake and the Town Roads which lie around it in a tangle at the western end of the town.

As the years passed, I became more and more interested in—almost entranced by—the secret life of this town, by the hidden relationships which seemed to come clearer and clearer to me. Much of this history remains either unwritten or unpublished: how the late Sheriff George Bannerman lost his virginity in the back seat of his dead father's car, how Ophelia Todd's husband was killed by a walking windmill, how Deputy Andy Clutterbuck lost the index finger on his left hand (it was cut off in a fan and the family dog ate it).

Following *The Dead Zone,* which is partly the story of the psychotic Frank Dodd, I wrote a novella called "The Body"; *Cujo,* the novel in which good old Sheriff Bannerman bit the dust; and a number of short stories and novelettes about the town (the best of them, at least in my mind, are "Mrs. Todd's Shortcut" and "Uncle Otto's Truck"). All of which is very well, but a state of entrancement with a fictional setting may not be the best thing in the world for a writer. It was for Faulkner and J. R. R. Tolkien, but sometimes a couple of exceptions just prove the rule, and besides, I don't play in that league.

So at some point I decided—first in my subconscious mind, I think, where all that Really Serious Work takes place—that the time had come to close the book on Castle Rock, Maine, where so many of my own favorite characters have lived and died. Enough, after all, is enough. Time to move on (maybe all the way next door to Harlow, ha-ha). But I didn't just want to walk away; I wanted to *finish* things, and do it with a bang.

Little by little I began to grasp how that could be done, and over the last four years or so I have been engaged in writing a

Castle Rock Trilogy, if you please—the *last* Castle Rock stories. They were not written in order (I sometimes think "out of order" is the story of my life), but now they *are* written, and they are serious enough . . . but I hope that doesn't mean that they are sober-sided or boring.

The first of these stories, *The Dark Half,* was published in 1989. While it is primarily the story of Thad Beaumont and is in large part set in a town called Ludlow (the town where the Creeds lived in *Pet Sematary*), the town of Castle Rock figures in the tale, and the book serves to introduce Sheriff Bannerman's replacement, a fellow named Alan Pangborn. Sheriff Pangborn is at the center of the last story in this sequence, a long novel called *Needful Things,* which is scheduled to be published next year and will conclude my doings with what local people call The Rock.

The connective tissue between these longer works is the story which follows. You will meet few if any of Castle Rock's larger figures in "The Sun Dog," but it will serve to introduce you to Pop Merrill, whose nephew is town bad boy (and Gordie LaChance's *bête noire* in "The Body") Ace Merrill. "The Sun Dog" also sets the stage for the final fireworks display . . . and, I hope, exists as a satisfying story on its own, one that can be read with pleasure even if you don't give a hang about *The Dark Half* or *Needful Things.*

One other thing needs to be said: every story has its own secret life, quite separate from its setting, and "The Sun Dog" is a story about cameras and photographs. About five years ago, my wife, Tabitha, became interested in photography, discovered she was good at it, and began to pursue it in a serious way, through study, experiment, and practice-practice-practice. I myself take bad photos (I'm one of those guys who always manage to cut off my subjects' heads, get pictures of them with their mouths hanging open, or both), but I have a great deal of respect for those who take good ones . . . and the whole process fascinates me.

In the course of her experiments, my wife got a Polaroid camera, a simple one accessible even to a doofus like me. I became fascinated with this camera. I had seen and used Polaroids before, of course, but I had never really *thought* about them much, nor had I ever looked closely at the images these cameras produce. The more I thought about them, the stranger they seemed. They are, after all, not just images but moments of time . . . and there is something so *peculiar* about them.

This story came almost all at once one night in the summer of 1987, but the thinking which made it possible went on for almost a year. And that's enough out of me, I think. It's been great to be with all of you again, but that doesn't mean I'm letting you go home just yet.

I think we have a birthday party to attend in the little town of Castle Rock.

CHAPTER ONE

September 15th was Kevin's birthday, and he got exactly what he wanted: a Sun.

The Kevin in question was Kevin Delevan, the birthday was his fifteenth, and the Sun was a Sun 660, a Polaroid camera which does everything for the novice photographer except make bologna sandwiches.

There *were* other gifts, of course; his sister, Meg, gave him a pair of mittens she had knitted herself, there was ten dollars from his grandmother in Des Moines, and his Aunt Hilda sent—as she always did—a string tie with a horrible clasp. She had sent the first of these when Kevin was three, which meant he already had twelve unused string ties with horrible clasps in a drawer of his bureau, to which this would be added—lucky thirteen. He had never worn any of them but was not allowed to throw them away. Aunt Hilda lived in Portland. She had never come to one of Kevin's or Meg's birthday parties, but she might decide to do just that one of these years. God knew she *could*; Portland was only fifty miles south of Castle Rock. And suppose she *did* come . . . and asked to see Kevin in one of his *other* ties (or Meg in one of her other scarves, for that matter)? With some relatives, an excuse might do. Aunt Hilda, however, was different. Aunt Hilda presented a certain golden possibility at a point where two essential facts about her crossed: she was Rich, and she was Old.

Someday, Kevin's Mom was convinced, she might DO SOME-THING for Kevin and Meg. It was understood that the SOME-THING would probably come after Aunt Hilda finally kicked it, in the form of a clause in her will. In the meantime, it was

1

thought wise to keep the horrible string ties and the equally horrible scarves. So this thirteenth string tie (on the clasp of which was a bird Kevin thought was a woodpecker) would join the others, and Kevin would write Aunt Hilda a thank-you note, not because his mother would insist on it and not because he thought or even cared that Aunt Hilda might DO SOMETHING for him and his kid sister someday, but because he was a generally thoughtful boy with good habits and no real vices.

He thanked his family for all his gifts (his mother and father had, of course, supplied a number of lesser ones, although the Polaroid was clearly the centerpiece, and they were delighted with *his* delight), not forgetting to give Meg a kiss (she giggled and pretended to rub it off but her own delight was equally clear) and to tell her he was sure the mittens would come in handy on the ski team this winter—but most of his attention was reserved for the Polaroid box, and the extra film packs which had come with it.

He was a good sport about the birthday cake and the ice cream, although it was clear he was itching to get at the camera and try it out. And as soon as he decently could, he did.

That was when the trouble started.

He read the instruction booklet as thoroughly as his eagerness to begin would allow, then loaded the camera while the family watched with anticipation and unacknowledged dread (for some reason, the gifts which seem the most wanted are the ones which so often don't work). There was a little collective sigh—more puff than gust—when the camera obediently spat out the cardboard square on top of the film packet, just as the instruction booklet had promised it would.

There were two small dots, one red and one green, separated by a zig-zag lightning-bolt on the housing of the camera. When Kevin loaded the camera, the red light came on. It stayed on for a couple of seconds. The family watched in silent fascination as the Sun 660 sniffed for light. Then the red light went out and the green light began to blink rapidly.

"It's ready," Kevin said, in the same straining-to-be-off-hand-but-not-quite-making-it tone with which Neil Armstrong had reported his first step upon the surface of Luna. "Why don't all you guys stand together?"

"I hate having my picture taken!" Meg cried, covering her face with the theatrical anxiety and pleasure which only sub-teenage girls and really bad actresses can manage.

"Come on, Meg," Mr. Delevan said.

"Don't be a goose, Meg," Mrs. Delevan said.

Meg dropped her hands (and her objections), and the three of them stood at the end of the table with the diminished birthday cake in the foreground.

Kevin looked through the viewfinder. "Squeeze a little closer to Meg, Mom," he said, motioning with his left hand. "You too, Dad." This time he motioned with his right.

"You're *squishing* me!" Meg said to her parents.

Kevin put his finger on the button which would fire the camera, then remembered a briefly glimpsed note in the instructions about how easy it was to cut off your subjects' heads in a photograph. *Off with their heads,* he thought, and it should have been funny, but for some reason he felt a little tingle at the base of his spine, gone and forgotten almost before it was noticed. He raised the camera a little. There. They were all in the frame. Good.

"Okay!" he sang. "Smile and say Intercourse!"

"Kevin!" his mother cried out.

His father burst out laughing, and Meg screeched the sort of mad laughter not even bad actresses often essay; girls between the ages of ten and twelve own sole title to that particular laugh.

Kevin pushed the button.

The flashbulb, powered by the battery in the film pack, washed the room in a moment of righteous white light.

It's mine, Kevin thought, and it should have been the surpassing moment of his fifteenth birthday. Instead, the thought brought back that odd little tingle. It was more noticeable this time.

The camera made a noise, something between a squeal and a whirr, a sound just a little beyond description but familiar enough to most people, just the same: the sound of a Polaroid camera squirting out what may not be art but what is often serviceable and almost always provides instant gratification.

"Lemme see it!" Meg cried.

"Hold your horses, muffin," Mr. Delevan said. "They take a little time to develop."

Meg was staring at the stiff gray surface of what was not yet a photograph with the rapt attention of a woman gazing into a crystal ball.

The rest of the family gathered around, and there was that same feeling of anxiety which had attended the ceremony of Loading the Camera: still life of the American Family waiting to let out its breath.

Kevin felt a terrible tenseness stealing into his muscles, and this time there was no question of ignoring it. He could not explain it . . . but it was there. He could not seem to take his eyes from that solid gray square within the white frame which would form the borders of the photograph.

"I think I see me!" Meg cried brightly. Then, a moment later: "No. I guess I don't. I think I see—"

They watched in utter silence as the gray cleared, as the mists are reputed to do in a seer's crystal when the vibrations or feelings or whatever they are are right, and the picture became visible to them.

Mr. Delevan was the first to break the silence.

"What is this?" he asked no one in particular. "Some kind of joke?"

Kevin had absently put the camera down rather too close to the edge of the table in order to watch the picture develop. Meg saw what the picture was and took a single step away. The expression on her face was neither fright nor awe but just ordinary surprise. One of her hands came up as she turned toward her father. The rising hand struck the camera and knocked it off the table and onto the floor. Mrs. Delevan had been looking at the emerging picture in a kind of trance, the expression on her face either that of a woman who is deeply puzzled or who is feeling the onset of a migraine headache. The sound of the camera hitting the floor startled her. She uttered a little scream and recoiled. In doing this, she tripped over Meg's foot and lost her balance. Mr. Delevan reached for her, propelling Meg, who was still between them, forward again, quite forcefully. Mr. Delevan not only caught his wife, but did so with some grace; for a moment they would have made a pretty picture indeed: Mom and Dad, showing they still know how to Cut A Rug, caught at the end of a spirited tango, she with one hand thrown up and her back deeply bowed, he bent over her in that ambiguous male posture which may be seen, when divorced from circumstance, as either solicitude or lust.

Meg was eleven, and less graceful. She went flying back toward the table and smacked into it with her stomach. The hit was hard enough to have injured her, but for the last year and a half she had been taking ballet lessons at the YWCA three afternoons a week. She did not dance with much grace, but she enjoyed ballet, and the dancing had fortunately toughened the muscles of her stomach enough for them to absorb the blow as efficiently as good shock absorbers absorb the pounding a road full of potholes can administer to a car. Still, there was a band of black and blue just above her hips the next day. These bruises took almost two weeks to first purple, then yellow, then fade . . . like a Polaroid picture in reverse.

At the moment this Rube Goldberg accident happened, she didn't even feel it; she simply banged into the table and cried out. The table tipped. The birthday cake, which should have been in the foreground of Kevin's first picture with his new camera, slid off the table. Mrs. Delevan didn't even have time to start her *Meg, are you all right?* before the remaining half of the cake fell on top of the Sun 660 with a juicy *splat!* that sent frosting all over their shoes and the baseboard of the wall.

The viewfinder, heavily smeared with Dutch chocolate, peered out like a periscope. That was all.

Happy birthday, Kevin.

Kevin and Mr. Delevan were sitting on the couch in the living room that evening when Mrs. Delevan came in, waving two dog-eared sheets of paper which had been stapled together. Kevin and Mr. Delevan both had open books in their laps (*The Best and the Brightest* for the father; *Shoot-Out at Laredo* for the son), but what they were mostly doing was staring at the Sun camera, which sat in disgrace on the coffee table amid a litter of Polaroid pictures. All the pictures appeared to show exactly the same thing.

Meg was sitting on the floor in front of them, using the VCR to watch a rented movie. Kevin wasn't sure which one it was, but there were a lot of people running around and screaming, so he guessed it was a horror picture. Megan had a passion for them. Both parents considered this a low taste (Mr. Delevan in particular was often outraged by what he called "that useless junk"), but tonight neither of them had said a word. Kevin guessed they were just grateful she had quit complaining about her bruised stomach and wondering aloud what the exact symptoms of a ruptured spleen might be.

"Here they are," Mrs. Delevan said. "I found them at the bottom of my purse the second time through." She handed the papers—a sales slip from J. C. Penney's and a Master-Card receipt—to her husband. "I can never find anything like this the first time. I don't think anyone can. It's like a law of nature."

She surveyed her husband and son, hands on her hips.

"You two look like someone just killed the family cat."

"We don't *have* a cat," Kevin said.

"Well, you know what I mean. It's a shame, of course, but

we'll get it sorted out in no time. Penney's will be happy to exchange it—"

"I'm not so sure of that," John Delevan said. He picked up the camera, looked at it with distaste (almost sneered at it, in fact), and then set it down again. "It got chipped when it hit the floor. See?"

Mrs. Delevan took only a cursory glance. "Well, if Penney's won't, I'm positive that the Polaroid company *will*. I mean, the fall obviously didn't cause whatever is wrong with it. The first picture looked just like all these, and Kevin took *that* one before Meg knocked it off the table."

"I didn't mean to," Meg said without turning around. On the screen, a pint-sized figure—a malevolent doll named Chucky, if Kevin had it right—was chasing a small boy. Chucky was dressed in blue overalls and waving a knife.

"I know, dear. How's your stomach?"

"Hurts," Meg said. "A little ice cream might help. Is there any left over?"

"Yes, I think so."

Meg gifted her mother with her most winning smile. "Would you get some for me?"

"Not at all," Mrs. Delevan said pleasantly. "Get it yourself. And what's that horrible thing you're watching?"

"Child's Play," Megan said. "There's this doll named Chucky that comes to life. It's neat."

Mrs. Delevan wrinkled her nose.

"Dolls don't come to life, Meg," her father said. He spoke heavily, as if knowing this was a lost cause.

"Chucky did," Meg said. "In movies, anything can happen." She used the remote control to freeze the movie and went to get her ice cream.

"Why does she want to watch that crap?" Mr. Delevan asked his wife, almost plaintively.

"I don't know, dear."

Kevin had picked up the camera in one hand and several of

7

the exposed Polaroids in the other—they had taken almost a dozen in all. "I'm not so sure I *want* a refund," he said.

His father stared at him. "*What?* Jesus wept!"

"Well," Kevin said, a little defensively, "I'm just saying that maybe we ought to think about it. I mean, it's not exactly an ordinary defect, is it? I mean, if the pictures came out over-exposed . . . or underexposed . . . or just plain blank . . . that would be one thing. But how do you get a thing like this? The same picture, over and over? I mean, look! And they're outdoors, even though we took every one of these pictures inside!"

"It's a practical joke," his father said. "It must be. The thing to do is just exchange the damned thing and forget about it."

"I don't think it's a practical joke," Kevin said. "First, it's too *complicated* to be a practical joke. How do you rig a camera to take the same picture over and over? Plus, the psychology is all wrong."

"Psychology, yet," Mr. Delevan said, rolling his eyes at his wife.

"Yes, psychology!" Kevin replied firmly. "When a guy loads your cigarette or hands you a stick of pepper gum, he hangs around to watch the fun, doesn't he? But unless you or Mom have been pulling my leg—"

"Your father isn't much of a leg-puller, dear," Mrs. Delevan said, stating the obvious gently.

Mr. Delevan was looking at Kevin with his lips pressed together. It was the look he always got when he perceived his son drifting toward that area of the ballpark where Kevin seemed most at home: left field. *Far* left field. There was a hunchy, intuitive streak in Kevin that had always puzzled and confounded him. He didn't know where it had come from, but he was sure it hadn't been *his* side of the family.

He sighed and looked at the camera again. A piece of black plastic had been chipped from the left side of the housing, and there was a crack, surely no thicker than a human hair, down the center of the viewfinder lens. The crack was so thin it disappeared completely when you raised the camera to your eye to set the shot you would not get—what you *would* get was on the coffee table, and there were nearly a dozen other examples in the dining room.

What you got was something that looked like a refugee from the local animal shelter.

"All right, what in the devil are you going to do with it?" he asked. "I mean, let's think this over reasonably, Kevin. What practical good is a camera that takes the same picture over and over?"

But it was not practical good Kevin was thinking about. In fact, he was not thinking at all. He was feeling . . . and remembering. In the instant when he had pushed the shutter release, one clear idea

(*it's mine*)

had filled his mind as completely as the momentary white flash had filled his eyes. That idea, complete yet somehow inexplicable, had been accompanied by a powerful mixture of emotions which he could still not identify completely . . . but he thought fear and excitement had predominated.

And besides—his father *always* wanted to look at things reasonably. He would never be able to understand Kevin's intuitions or Meg's interest in killer dolls named Chucky.

Meg came back in with a huge dish of ice cream and started the movie again. Someone was now attempting to toast Chucky with a blowtorch, but he went right on waving his knife. "Are you two still arguing?"

"We're having a discussion," Mr. Delevan said. His lips were pressed more tightly together than ever.

"Yeah, right," Meg said, sitting down on the floor again and crossing her legs. "You always say that."

"Meg?" Kevin said kindly.

"What?"

"If you dump that much ice cream on top of a ruptured

spleen, you'll die horribly in the night. Of course, your spleen might not actually be ruptured, but—"

Meg stuck her tongue out at him and turned back to the movie.

Mr. Delevan was looking at his son with an expression of mingled affection and exasperation. "Look, Kev—it's your camera. No argument about that. You can do whatever you want with it. But—"

"Dad, aren't you even the least bit interested in *why* it's doing what it's doing?"

"Nope," John Delevan said.

It was Kevin's turn to roll his eyes. Meanwhile, Mrs. Delevan was looking from one to the other like someone who is enjoying a pretty good tennis match. Nor was this far from the truth. She had spent years watching her son and her husband sharpen themselves on each other, and she was not bored with it yet. She sometimes wondered if they would ever discover how much alike they really were.

"Well, I want to think it over."

"Fine. I just want *you* to know that I can swing by Penney's tomorrow and exchange the thing—if you want me to and they agree to swap a piece of chipped merchandise, that is. If you want to keep it, that's fine, too. I wash my hands of it." He dusted his palms briskly together to illustrate.

"I suppose you don't want *my* opinion," Meg said.

"Right," Kevin said.

"Of course we do, Meg," Mrs. Delevan said.

"I think it's a supernatural camera," Meg said. She licked ice cream from her spoon. "I think it's a Manifestation."

"That's utterly ridiculous," Mr. Delevan said at once.

"No, it's not," Meg said. "It happens to be the only explanation that fits. You just don't think so because you don't believe in stuff like that. If a ghost ever floated up to you, Dad, you wouldn't even see it. What do you think, Kev?"

For a moment Kevin didn't—couldn't—answer. He felt

as if another flashbulb had gone off, this one behind his eyes instead of in front of them.

"Kev? Earth to Kevin!"

"I think you might just have something there, squirt," he said slowly.

"Oh my dear God," John Delevan said, getting up. "It's the revenge of Freddy and Jason—my kid thinks his birthday camera's haunted. I'm going to bed, but before I do, I want to say just one more thing. A camera that takes photographs of the same thing over and over again—especially something as ordinary as what's in *these* pictures—is a *boring* manifestation of the supernatural."

"Still . . ." Kevin said. He held up the photos like a dubious poker hand.

"I think it's time we all went to bed," Mrs. Delevan said briskly. "Meg, if you absolutely need to finish that cinematic masterpiece, you can do it in the morning."

"But it's almost over!" Meg cried.

"I'll come up with her, Mom," Kevin said, and, fifteen minutes later, with the malevolent Chucky disposed of (at least until the sequel), he did. But sleep did not come easily for Kevin that night. He lay long awake in his bedroom, listening to a strong late-summer wind rustle the leaves outside into whispery conversation, thinking about what might make a camera take the same picture over and over and over again, and what such a thing might mean. He only began to slip toward sleep when he realized his decision had been made: he would keep the Polaroid Sun at least a little while longer.

It's mine, he thought again. He rolled over on his side, closed his eyes, and was sleeping deeply forty seconds later.

CHAPTER TWO

Amid the tickings and tockings of what sounded like at least fifty thousand clocks and totally undisturbed by them, Reginald "Pop" Merrill shone a pencil-beam of light from a gadget even more slender than a doctor's ophthalmoscope into Kevin's Polaroid 660 while Kevin stood by. Pop's eyeglasses, which he didn't need for close work, were propped on the bald dome of his head.

"Uh-huh," he said, and clicked the light off.

"Does that mean you know what's wrong with it?" Kevin asked.

"Nope," Pop Merrill said, and snapped the Sun's film compartment, now empty, closed. "Don't have a clue." And before Kevin could say anything else, the clocks began to strike four o'clock, and for a few moments conversation, although possible, seemed absurd.

I want to think it over, he had told his father on the evening he had turned fifteen—three days ago now—and it was a statement which had surprised both of them. As a child he had made a career of *not* thinking about things, and Mr. Delevan had in his heart of hearts come to believe Kevin never *would* think about things, whether he ought to or not. They had been seduced, as fathers and sons often are, by the idea that their behavior and very different modes of thinking would never change, thus fixing their relationship eternally . . . and childhood would thus go on forever. *I want to think it over:* there was a world of potential change implicit in that statement.

Further, as a human being who had gone through his life to that point making most decisions on instinct rather than reason (and he was one of those lucky ones whose instincts were almost always good—the sort of person, in other words, who drives reasonable people mad), Kevin was surprised and intrigued to find that he was actually On the Horns of a Dilemma.

Horn #1: he had wanted a Polaroid camera and he had gotten one for his birthday, but, dammit, he had wanted a Polaroid camera that *worked.*

Horn #2: he was deeply intrigued by Meg's use of the word *supernatural.*

His younger sister had a daffy streak a mile wide, but she wasn't stupid, and Kevin didn't think she had used the word lightly or thoughtlessly. His father, who was of the Reasonable rather than Instinctive tribe, had scoffed, but Kevin found he wasn't ready to go and do likewise . . . at least, not yet. That word. That fascinating, exotic word. It became a plinth which his mind couldn't help circling.

I think it's a Manifestation.

Kevin was amused (and a little chagrined) that only Meg had been smart enough—or brave enough—to actually say what should have occurred to all of them, given the oddity of the pictures the Sun produced, but in truth, it wasn't really that amazing. They were not a religious family; they went to church on the Christmas Day every third year when Aunt Hilda came to spend the holiday with them instead of her other remaining relatives, but except for the occasional wedding or funeral, that was about all. If any of them truly believed in the invisible world it was Megan, who couldn't get enough of walking corpses, living dolls, and cars that came to life and ran down people they didn't like.

Neither of Kevin's parents had much taste for the bizarre. They didn't read their horoscopes in the daily paper; they would never mistake comets or falling stars for signs from the Almighty; where one couple might see the face of Jesus on the bottom of an enchilada, John and Mary Delevan would see only an overcooked enchilada. It was not surprising that Kevin, who had never seen the man in the moon because neither mother nor father had bothered to point it out to him, had been likewise unable to see the possibility of *a supernatural Manifestation* in a camera which took the same picture over and over again, inside or outside, even in the dark of his bedroom closet, until it was suggested to him by his sister, who had once written a fan-letter to Jason and gotten an autographed glossy photo of a guy in a bloodstained hockey mask by return mail.

Once the possibility *had* been pointed out, it became difficult to unthink; as Dostoyevsky, that smart old Russian, once said to his little brother when the two of them were both smart *young* Russians, try to spend the next thirty seconds *not* thinking of a blue-eyed polar bear.

It was hard to do.

So he had spent two days circling that plinth in his mind, trying to read hieroglyphics that weren't even *there*, for pity's sake, and trying to decide which he wanted more: the camera or the possibility of a Manifestation. Or, put another way, whether he wanted the Sun . . . or the man in the moon.

By the end of the second day (even in fifteen-year-olds who are clearly destined for the Reasonable tribe, dilemmas rarely last longer than a week), he had decided to take the man in the moon . . . on a trial basis, at least.

He came to this decision in study hall period seven, and when the bell rang, signalling the end of both the study hall and the school-day, he had gone to the teacher he respected most, Mr. Baker, and had asked him if he knew of anyone who repaired cameras.

"Not like a regular camera-shop guy," he explained. "More like a . . . you know . . . a thoughtful guy."

"An F-stop philosopher?" Mr. Baker asked. His saying things like that was one of the reasons why Kevin respected him. It was just a cool thing to say. "A sage of the shutter? An alchemist of the aperture? A—"

"A guy who's seen a lot," Kevin said cagily.

"Pop Merrill," Mr. Baker said.

"Who?"

"He runs the Emporium Galorium."

"Oh. *That* place."

"Yeah," Mr. Baker said, grinning. "*That* place. If, that is, what you're looking for is a sort of homespun Mr. Fixit."

"I guess that's what I am looking for."

"He's got damn near everything in there," Mr. Baker said, and Kevin could agree with that. Even though he had never actually been inside, he passed the Emporium Galorium five, ten, maybe fifteen times a week (in a town the size of Castle Rock, you had to pass *everything* a lot, and it got amazingly boring in Kevin Delevan's humble opinion), and he had looked in the windows. It seemed crammed literally to the rafters with objects, most of them mechanical. But his mother called it "a junk-store" in a sniffing voice, and his father said Mr. Merrill made his money "rooking the summer people," and so Kevin had never gone in. If it had *only* been a "junk-store," he might have; almost certainly would have, in fact. But doing what the summer people did, or buying something where summer people "got rooked" was unthinkable. He would be as apt to wear a blouse and skirt to high school. Summer people could do what they wanted (and did). They were all mad, and conducted their affairs in a mad fashion. *Exist* with them, fine. But be *confused* with them? No. No. And no *sir.*

"Damn near everything," Mr. Baker repeated, "and most of what he's got, he fixed himself. He thinks that crackerbarrel philosopher act he does—glasses up on top of the head, wise pronouncements, all of that—fools people. No one who knows him disabuses him. I'm not sure anyone would *dare* disabuse him."

"Why? What do you mean?"

Mr. Baker shrugged. An odd, tight little smile touched his mouth. "Pop—Mr. Merrill, I mean—has got his fingers in a lot of pies around here. You'd be surprised, Kevin."

Kevin didn't care about how many pies Pop Merrill was currently fingering, or what their fillings might be. He was left with only one more important question, since the summer people were gone and he could probably slink into the Emporium Galorium unseen tomorrow afternoon if he took advantage of the rule which allowed all students but freshmen to cut their last-period study hall twice a month.

"Do I call him Pop or Mr. Merrill?"

Solemnly, Mr. Baker replied, "I think the man kills anyone under the age of sixty who calls him Pop."

And the thing was, Kevin had an idea Mr. Baker wasn't exactly joking.

"You really don't know, huh?" Kevin said when the clocks began to wind down.

It had not been like in a movie, where they all start and finish striking at once; these were real clocks, and he guessed that most of them—along with the rest of the appliances in the Emporium Galorium—were not really running at all but sort of lurching along. They had begun at what his own Seiko quartz watch said was 3:58. They began to pick up speed and volume gradually (like an old truck fetching second gear with a tired groan and jerk). There were maybe four seconds when all of them really *did* seem to be striking, bonging, chiming, clanging, and cuckoo-ing at the same time, but four seconds was all the synchronicity they could manage. And "winding down" was not exactly what they did. What they did was sort of give up, like water finally consenting to gurgle its way down a drain which is almost but not quite completely plugged.

He didn't have any idea why he was so disappointed. Had he really expected anything else? For Pop Merrill, whom Mr. Baker had described as a crackerbarrel philosopher and home-spun Mr. Fixit, to pull out a spring and say, "Here it is—this is the bastard causing that dog to show up every time you push the shutter release. It's a dog-spring, belongs in one of those toy dogs a kid winds up so it'll walk and bark a little, some joker on the Polaroid Sun 660 assembly line's *always* putting them in the damn cameras."

Had he expected that?

No. But he had expected . . . *something.*

"Don't have a friggin clue," Pop repeated cheerfully. He reached behind him and took a Douglas MacArthur corncob pipe from a holder shaped like a bucket seat. He began to tamp tobacco into it from an imitation-leather pouch with the words EVIL WEED stamped into it. "Can't even take these babies apart, you know."

"You can't?"

"Nope," Pop said. He was just as chipper as a bird. He paused long enough to hook a thumb over the wire ridge between the lenses of his rimless specs and give them a yank. They dropped off his bald dome and fell neatly into place, hiding the red spots on the sides of his nose, with a fleshy little thump. "You could take apart the old ones," he went on, now producing a Diamond Blue Tip match from a pocket of his vest (of course he was wearing a vest) and pressing the thick yellow thumbnail of his right hand on its head. Yes, this was a man who could rook the summer people with one hand tied behind his back (always assuming it wasn't the one he used to first fish out his matches and then light them)—even at fifteen years of age, Kevin could see that. Pop Merrill had *style.* "The Polaroid Land cameras, I mean. Ever seen one of those beauties?"

"No," Kevin said.

Pop snapped the match alight on the first try, which of course he would always do, and applied it to the corncob, his words sending out little smoke-signals which looked pretty and smelled absolutely foul.

"Oh yeah," he said. "They looked like those old-time cameras people like Mathew Brady used before the turn of the century—or before the Kodak people introduced the Brownie box camera, anyway. What I mean to say is" (Kevin was rapidly learning that this was Pop Merrill's favorite phrase; he used it the way some of the kids in school used "you know," as intensifier, modifier, qualifier, and most of all as a convenient thought-gathering pause) "they tricked it up some, put on chrome and real leather side-panels, but it still looked old-fashioned, like the sort of camera folks used to make daguerreotypes with. When you opened one of those old Polaroid Land cameras, it snapped out an accordion neck, because the lens needed half a foot, maybe even nine inches, to focus the image. It looked old-fashioned as hell when you put it next to one of the Kodaks in the late forties and early fifties, and it was like those old daguerreotype cameras in another way—it only took black-and-white photos."

"Is that so?" Kevin asked, interested in spite of himself.

"Oh, ayuh!" Pop said, chipper as a chickadee, blue eyes twinkling at Kevin through the smoke from his fuming stewpot of a pipe and from behind his round rimless glasses. It was the sort of twinkle which may indicate either good humor or avarice. "What I mean to say is that people laughed at those cameras the way they laughed at the Volkswagen Beetles when *they* first come out . . . but they bought the Polaroids just like they bought the VWs. Because the Beetles got good gas mileage and didn't go bust so often as American cars, and the Polaroids did one thing the Kodaks and even the Nikons and Minoltas and Leicas didn't."

"Took instant pictures."

Pop smiled. "Well . . . not exactly. What I mean to say is you took your pitcher, and then you yanked on this flap to pull it out. It didn't have no motor, didn't make that squidgy little whining noise like modern Polaroids."

So there *was* a perfect way to describe that sound after all, it was just that you had to find a Pop Merrill to tell it to you: the sound that Polaroid cameras made when they spat out their product was *a squidgy little whine.*

"Then you had to time her," Pop said.

"Time—?"

"Oh, ayuh!" Pop said with great relish, bright as the early bird who has found that fabled worm. "What I mean to say is they didn't have none of this happy automatic crappy back in those days. You yanked and out come this long strip which you put on the table or whatever and timed off sixty seconds on your watch. Had to be sixty, or right around there, anyway. Less and you'd have an underexposed pitcher. More and it'd be overexposed."

"Wow," Kevin said respectfully. And this was not bogus respect, jollying the old man along in hopes he would get back to the point, which was not a bunch of long-dead cameras that had been wonders in their day but his *own* camera, the damned balky Sun 660 sitting on Pop's worktable with the guts of an old seven-day clock on its right and something which looked suspiciously like a dildo on its left. It wasn't bogus respect and Pop knew it, and it occurred to Pop (it wouldn't have to Kevin) how fleeting that great white god "state-of-the-art" really was; ten years, he thought, and the phrase itself would be gone. From the boy's fascinated expression, you would have thought he was hearing about something as antique as George Washington's wooden dentures instead of a camera everyone had thought was the ultimate only thirty-five years ago. But of course this boy had still been circling around in the unhatched void thirty-five years ago, part of a female who hadn't yet even met the male who would provide his other half.

"What I mean to say is it was a regular little darkroom goin on in there between the pitcher and the backing," Pop resumed, slow at first but speeding up as his own mostly genuine interest in the subject resurfaced (but the thoughts of who this kid's father was and what the kid might be worth to him and the strange thing the kid's camera was up to never completely left his mind). "And at the end of the minute, you peeled the pitcher off the back—had to be careful when you did it, too, because there was all this goo like jelly on the back,

19

and if your skin was in the least bit sensitive, you could get a pretty good burn."

"Awesome," Kevin said. His eyes were wide, and now he looked like a kid hearing about the old two-holer outhouses which Pop and all his childhood colleagues (they were almost all colleagues; he had had few childhood friends in Castle Rock, perhaps preparing even then for his life's work of rooking the summer people and the other children somehow sensing it, like a faint smell of skunk) had taken for granted, doing your business as fast as you could in high summer because one of the wasps always circling around down there between the manna and the two holes which were the heaven from which the manna fell might at any time take a notion to plant its stinger in one of your tender little boycheeks, and also doing it as fast as you could in deep winter because your tender little boycheeks were apt to freeze solid if you didn't. *Well*, Pop thought, *so much for the Camera of the Future. Thirty-five years and to this kid it's interestin in the same way a backyard shithouse is interestin.*

"The negative was on the back," Pop said. "And your positive—well, it was black and white, but it was *fine* black and white. It was just as crisp and clear as you'd ever want even today. And you had this little pink thing, about as long as a school eraser, as I remember; it squeegeed out some kind of chemical, smelled like ether, and you had to rub it over the pitcher as fast as you could, or that pitcher'd roll right up, like the tube in the middle of a roll of bung-fodder."

Kevin burst out laughing, tickled by these pleasant antiquities.

Pop quit long enough to get his pipe going again. When he had, he resumed: "A camera like that, nobody but the Polaroid people really knew what it was doing—I mean to say those people were *close*—but it was *mechanical*. You could take it *apart*."

He looked at Kevin's Sun with some distaste.

20

"And, lots of times when one went bust, that was as much as you needed. Fella'd come in with one of those and say it wouldn't work, moanin about how he'd have to send it back to the Polaroid people to get it fixed and that'd prob'ly take months and would I take a look. 'Well,' I'd say, 'prob'ly nothin I can do, what I mean to say is nobody really knows about these cameras but the Polaroid people and they're goddam close, but I'll take a look.' All the time knowin it was prob'ly just a loose screw inside that shutter-housin or maybe a fouled spring, or hell, maybe Junior slathered some peanut butter in the film compartment."

One of his bright bird-eyes dropped in a wink so quick and so marvellously sly that, Kevin thought, if you hadn't known he was talking about summer people, you would have thought it was your paranoid imagination, or, more likely, missed it entirely.

"What I mean to say is you had your perfect situation," Pop said. "If you could fix it, you were a goddam wonder-worker. Why, I have put eight dollars and fifty cents in my pocket for takin a couple of little pieces of potato-chip out from between the trigger and the shutter-spring, my son, and the woman who brought that camera in kissed me on the lips. Right . . . on . . . the lips."

Kevin observed Pop's eye drop momentarily closed again behind the semi-transparent mat of blue smoke.

"And of course, if it was somethin you couldn't fix, they didn't hold it against you because, what I mean to say, they never really expected you to be able to do nothin in the first place. You was only a last resort before they put her in a box and stuffed newspaper around her to keep her from bein broke even worse in the mail, and shipped her off to Schenectady.

"But—*this* camera." He spoke in the ritualistic tone of distaste all philosophers of the crackerbarrel, whether in Athens of the golden age or in a small-town junk-shop during this current one of brass, adopt to express their view of entropy with-

21

out having to come right out and state it. "Wasn't put together, son. What I mean to say is it was *poured*. I could maybe pop the lens, and will if you want me to, and I *did* look in the film compartment, although I knew I wouldn't see a goddam thing wrong—that I recognized, at least—and I didn't. But beyond that I can't go. I could take a hammer and wind it right to her, could *break* it, what I mean to say, but fix it?" He spread his hands in pipe-smoke. "Nossir."

"Then I guess I'll just have to—" *return it after all,* he meant to finish, but Pop broke in.

"Anyway, son, I think you knew that. What I mean to say is you're a bright boy, you can see when a thing's all of a piece. I don't think you brought that camera in to be *fixed*. I think you know that even if it *wasn't* all of a piece, a man couldn't fix what *that* thing's doing, at least not with a screwdriver. I think you brought it in to ask me if I knew what it's *up* to."

"Do you?" Kevin asked. He was suddenly tense all over.

"I might," Pop Merrill said calmly. He bent over the pile of photographs—twenty-eight of them now, counting the one Kevin had snapped to demonstrate, and the one Pop had snapped to demonstrate to himself. "These in order?"

"Not really. Pretty close, though. Does it matter?"

"I think so," Pop said. "They're a little bit different, ain't they? Not much, but a little."

"Yeah," Kevin said. "I can see the difference in *some* of them, but . . ."

"Do you know which one is the first? I could prob'ly figure it out for myself, but time is money, son."

"That's easy," Kevin said, and picked one out of the untidy little pile. "See the frosting?" He pointed at a small brown spot on the picture's white edging.

"Ayup." Pop didn't spare the dab of frosting more than a glance. He looked closely at the photograph, and after a moment he opened the drawer of his worktable. Tools were littered untidily about inside. To one side, in its own space, was an object wrapped in jeweler's velvet. Pop took this out, folded the cloth back, and removed a large magnifying glass with a switch in its base. He bent over the Polaroid and pushed the switch. A bright circle of light fell on the picture's surface.

"That's neat!" Kevin said.

"Ayup," Pop said again. Kevin could tell that for Pop he was no longer there. Pop was studying the picture closely.

If one had not known the odd circumstances of its taking, the picture would hardly have seemed to warrant such close scrutiny. Like most photographs which are taken with a decent camera, good film, and by a photographer at least intelligent enough to keep his finger from blocking the lens, it was clear, understandable . . . and, like so many Polaroids, oddly un-dramatic. It was a picture in which you could identify and name each object, but its content was as flat as its surface. It was not well composed, but composition wasn't what was wrong with it—that undramatic flatness could hardly be called *wrong* at all, any more than a real day in a real life could be called wrong because nothing worthy of even a made-for-television movie happened during its course. As in so many Polaroids, the things in the picture were only *there,* like an empty chair on a porch or an unoccupied child's swing in a backyard or a passengerless car sitting at an unremarkable curb without even a flat tire to make it interesting or unique.

What was wrong with the picture was the *feeling* that it was wrong. Kevin had remembered the sense of unease he had felt while composing his subjects for the picture he *meant* to take, and the ripple of gooseflesh up his back when, with the glare of the flashbulb still lighting the room, he had thought, *It's mine.* That was what was wrong, and as with the man in the moon you can't unsee once you've seen it, so, he was discovering, you couldn't *unfeel* certain feelings . . . and when it came to these pictures, those feelings were bad.

Kevin thought: *It's like there was a wind—very soft, very cold—blowing out of that picture.*

For the first time, the idea that it might be something supernatural—that this was part of a Manifestation—did something more than just intrigue him. For the first time he found himself wishing he had simply let this thing go. *It's mine*—that was what he had thought when his finger had pushed the shutter-button for the first time. Now he found himself wondering if maybe he hadn't gotten that backward.

I'm scared of it. Of what it's doing.

That made him mad, and he bent over Pop Merrill's shoulder, hunting as grimly as a man who has lost a diamond in a sandpile, determined that, no matter what he saw (always supposing he *should* see something new, and he didn't think he would; he had studied all these photographs often enough now to believe he had seen all there was to see in them), he would *look* at it, *study* it, and under no circumstances allow himself to unsee it. Even if he could . . . and a dolorous voice inside suggested very strongly that the time for unseeing was now past, possibly forever.

What the picture showed was a large black dog in front of a white picket fence. The picket fence wasn't going to be white much longer, unless someone in that flat Polaroid world painted or at least whitewashed it. That didn't seem likely; the fence looked untended, forgotten. The tops of some pickets were broken off. Others sagged loosely outward.

The dog was on a sidewalk in front of the fence. His hindquarters were to the viewer. His tail, long and bushy, drooped. He appeared to be smelling one of the fence-pickets—probably, Kevin thought, because the fence was what his dad called a "letter-drop," a place where many dogs would lift their legs and leave mystic yellow squirts of message before moving on.

The dog looked like a stray to Kevin. Its coat was long and tangled and sown with burdocks. One of its ears had the crumpled look of an old battle-scar. Its shadow trailed long enough to finish outside the frame on the weedy, patchy lawn inside the picket fence. The shadow made Kevin think the picture had been taken not long after dawn or not long before sunset; with no idea of the direction the photographer (*what* photographer, ha-ha) had been facing, it was impossible to tell which, just that he (or she) must have been standing only a few degrees shy of due east or west.

There was something in the grass at the far left of the picture which looked like a child's red rubber ball. It was inside the fence, and enough behind one of the lackluster clumps of grass so it was hard to tell.

And that was all.

"Do you recognize anything?" Pop asked, cruising his magnifying glass slowly back and forth over the photo's surface. Now the dog's hindquarters swelled to the size of hillocks tangled with wild and ominously exotic black undergrowth; now three or four of the scaly pickets became the size of old telephone poles; now, suddenly, the object behind the clump of grass clearly became a child's ball (although under Pop's glass it was as big as a soccer ball): Kevin could even see the stars which girdled its middle in upraised rubber lines. So something new *was* revealed under Pop's glass, and in a few moments Kevin would see something else himself, without it. But that was later.

"Jeez, no," Kevin said. "How could I, Mr. Merrill?"

"Because there are *things* here," Pop said patiently. His glass went on cruising. Kevin thought of a movie he had seen once where the cops sent out a searchlight-equipped helicopter to look for escaped prisoners. "A dog, a sidewalk, a picket fence that needs paintin or takin down, a lawn that needs tendin. The sidewalk ain't much—you can't even see all of it—and the house, even the foundation, ain't in the frame, but what I mean to say is there's that dog. You recognize *it?*"

"No."

"The fence?"

"No."

25

"What about that red rubber ball? What about that, son?"

"No . . . but you look like you think I should."

"I look like I thought you *might*," Pop said. "You never had a ball like that when you were a tyke?"

"Not that I remember, no."

"You got a sister, you said."

"Megan."

"She never had a ball like that?"

"I don't think so. I never took that much interest in Meg's toys. She had a BoLo bouncer once, and the ball on the end of it was red, but a different shade. Darker."

"Ayuh. I know what a ball like that looks like. This ain't one. And that mightn't be your lawn?"

"Jes—I mean jeepers, no." Kevin felt a little offended. He and his dad took good care of the lawn around their house. It was a deep green and would stay that way, even under the fallen leaves, until at least mid-October. "We don't have a picket fence, anyway." *And if we did,* he thought, *it wouldn't look like that mess.*

Pop let go of the switch in the base of the magnifying glass, placed it on the square of jeweler's velvet, and with a care which approached reverence folded the sides over it. He returned it to its former place in the drawer and closed the drawer. He looked at Kevin closely. He had put his pipe aside, and there was now no smoke to obscure his eyes, which were still sharp but not twinkling anymore.

"What I mean to say is, could it have been your house before you owned it, do you think? Ten years ago—"

"We owned it ten years ago," Kevin replied, bewildered.

"Well, twenty? Thirty? What I mean to say, do you recognize how the land lies? Looks like it climbs a little."

"Our front lawn—" He thought deeply, then shook his head. "No, ours is flat. If it does anything, it goes down a little. Maybe that's why the cellar ships a little water in a wet spring."

"Ayuh, ayuh, could be. What about the back lawn?"

"There's no sidewalk back there," Kevin said. "And on the sides—" He broke off. "You're trying to find out if my camera's taking pictures of the past!" he said, and for the first time he was really, actively frightened. He rubbed his tongue on the roof of his mouth and seemed to taste metal.

"I was just askin." Pop rapped his fingers beside the photographs, and when he spoke, it seemed to be more to himself than to Kevin. "You know," he said, "some goddam funny things seem to happen from time to time with two gadgets we've come to take pretty much for granted. I ain't sayin they *do* happen; only if they don't, there are a lot of liars and out-n-out hoaxers in the world."

"What gadgets?"

"Tape recorders and Polaroid cameras," Pop said, still seeming to talk to the pictures, or himself, and there was no Kevin in this dusty clock-drumming space at the back of the Emporium Galorium at all. "Take tape recorders. Do you know how many people claim to have recorded the voices of dead folks on tape recorders?"

"No," Kevin said. He didn't particularly mean for his own voice to come out hushed, but it did; he didn't seem to have a whole lot of air in his lungs to speak with, for some reason or other.

"Me neither," Pop said, stirring the photographs with one finger. It was blunt and gnarled, a finger which looked made for rude and clumsy motions and operations, for poking people and knocking vases off endtables and causing nosebleeds if it tried to do so much as hook a humble chunk of dried snot from one of its owner's nostrils. Yet Kevin had watched the man's hands and thought there was probably more grace in that one finger than in his sister Meg's entire body (and maybe in his own; Clan Delevan was not known for its light-footedness or -handedness, which was probably one reason why he thought that image of his father so nimbly catching his mother on the

27

way down had stuck with him, and might forever). Pop Merrill's finger looked as if it would at any moment sweep all the photographs onto the floor—by mistake; this sort of clumsy finger would always poke and knock and tweak by mistake—but it did not. The Polaroids seemed to barely stir in response to its restless movements.

Supernatural, Kevin thought again, and shivered a little. An *actual* shiver, surprising and dismaying and a little embarrassing even if Pop had not seen it.

"But there's even a way they do it," Pop said, and then, as if Kevin had asked: "Who? Damn if I know. I guess some of them are 'psychic investigators,' or at least call themselves that or some such, but I guess it's more'n likely most of em are just playin around, like folks that use Ouija Boards at parties."

He looked up at Kevin grimly, as if rediscovering him.

"You got a Ouija, son?"

"No."

"Ever played with one?"

"No."

"Don't," Pop said more grimly than ever. "Fucking things are dangerous."

Kevin didn't dare tell the old man he hadn't the slightest idea what a weegee board was.

"Anyway, they set up a tape machine to record in an empty room. It's supposed to be an old house, is what I mean to say, one with a History, if they can find it. Do you know what I mean when I say a house with a History, son?"

"I guess . . . like a haunted house?" Kevin hazarded. He found he was sweating lightly, as he had done last year every time Mrs. Whittaker announced a pop quiz in Algebra I.

"Well, that'll do. These . . . people . . . like it best if it's a house with a *Violent* History, but they'll take what they can get. Anyhow, they set up the machine and record that empty room. Then, the next day—they always do it at night, is what I mean to say, they ain't happy unless they can do it at night, and midnight if they can get it—the next day they play her back."

"An empty room?"

"Sometimes," Pop said in a musing voice that might or might not have disguised some deeper feeling, "there are voices."

Kevin shivered again. There were hieroglyphics on the plinth after all. Nothing you'd want to read, but . . . yeah. They were there.

"*Real* voices?"

"Usually imagination," Pop said dismissively. "But once or twice I've heard people I trust say they've heard real voices."

"But *you* never have?"

"Once," Pop said shortly, and said nothing else for so long Kevin was beginning to think he was done when he added, "It was one word. Clear as a bell. 'Twas recorded in the parlor of an empty house in Bath. Man killed his wife there in 1946."

"What was the word?" Kevin asked, knowing he would not be told just as surely as he knew no power on earth, certainly not his own willpower, could have kept him from asking.

But Pop *did* tell.

"Basin."

Kevin blinked. "Basin?"

"Ayuh."

"That doesn't mean anything."

"It might," Pop said calmly, "if you know he cut her throat and then held her head over a basin to catch the blood."

"Oh my God!"

"Ayuh."

"Oh my God, really?"

Pop didn't bother answering that.

"It couldn't have been a fake?"

Pop gestured with the stem of his pipe at the Polaroids. "Are those?"

"Oh my God."

"Polaroids, now," Pop said, like a narrator moving briskly

to a new chapter in a novel and reading the words *Meanwhile, in another part of the forest,* "I've seen pitchers with people in em that the other people in the pitcher swear weren't there with em when the pitcher was taken. And there's one—this is a famous one—that a lady took over in England. What she did was snap a pitcher of some fox-hunters comin back home at the end of the day. You see em, about twenty in all, comin over a little wooden bridge. It's a tree-lined country road on both sides of that bridge. The ones in front are off the bridge already. And over on the right of the pitcher, standin by the road, there's a lady in a long dress and a hat with a veil on it so you can't see her face and she's got her pocketbook over her arm. Why, you can even see she's wearin a locket on her boosom, or maybe it's a watch.

"Well, when the lady that took the pitcher saw it, she got wicked upset, and wasn't nobody could blame her, son, because what I mean to say is she meant to take a pitcher of those fox-hunters comin home and no one else, because there wasn't nobody else *there.* Except in the pitcher there is. And when you look real close, it seems like you can see the trees right through that lady."

He's making all this up, putting me on, and when I leave he'll have a great big horselaugh, Kevin thought, knowing Pop Merrill was doing nothing of the sort.

"The lady that took that pitcher was stayin at one of those big English homes like they have on the education-TV shows, and when she showed that pitcher, I heard the man of the house fainted dead away. That part could be made up. Prob'ly is. *Sounds* made up, don't it? But I seen that pitcher in an article next to a painted portrait of that fella's great-grandmother, and it could be her, all right. Can't tell for certain because of the veil. But it *could* be."

"Could be a hoax, too," Kevin said faintly.

"Could be," Pop said indifferently. "People get up to all

sorts of didos. Lookit my nephew, there, for instance, Ace."
Pop's nose wrinkled. "Doin four years in Shawshank, and for
what? Bustin into The Mellow Tiger. He got up to didos and
Sheriff Pangborn slammed him in the jug for it. Little ring-
meat got just what he deserved."

Kevin, displaying a wisdom far beyond his years, said nothing.

"But when ghosts show up in photographs, son—or, like
you say, what people *claim* to be ghosts—it's almost always
in *Polaroid* photographs. And it almost always seems to be
by accident. Now your pitchers of flyin saucers and that Lock
Nest Monster, they almost always show up in the other kind.
The kind some smart fella can get up to didos with in a darkroom."

He dropped Kevin a third wink, expressing all the didos
(whatever *they* were) an unscrupulous photographer might get
up to in a well-equipped darkroom.

Kevin thought of asking Pop if it was possible someone
could get up to didos with a weegee and decided to continue
keeping his mouth shut. It still seemed by far the wisest course.

"All by way of sayin I thought I'd ask if you saw somethin
you knew in *these* Polaroid pitchers."

"I don't, though," Kevin said so earnestly that he believed
Pop would believe he was lying, as his mom always did when
he made the tactical mistake of even controlled vehemence.

"Ayuh, ayuh," Pop said, believing him so dismissively
Kevin was almost irritated.

"Well," Kevin said after a moment which was silent except
for the fifty thousand ticking clocks, "I guess that's it, huh?"

"Maybe not," Pop said. "What I mean to say is I got me
a little idear. You mind takin some more pitchers with that
camera?"

"What good is it? They're all the same."

"That's the point. They ain't."

Kevin opened his mouth, then closed it.

"I'll even chip in for the film," Pop said, and when he saw the amazed look on Kevin's face he quickly qualified: "A little, anyway."

"How many pictures would you want?"

"Well, you got . . . what? Twenty-eight already, is that right?"

"Yes, I think so."

"Thirty more," Pop said after a moment's thought.

"Why?"

"Ain't gonna tell you. Not right now." He produced a heavy purse that was hooked to a belt-loop on a steel chain. He opened it and took out a ten-dollar bill, hesitated, and added two ones with obvious reluctance. "Guess that'd cover half of it."

Yeah, right, Kevin thought.

"If you really *are* int'rested in the trick that camera's doing, I guess you'd pony up the rest, wouldn't you?" Pop's eyes gleamed at him like the eyes of an old, curious cat.

Kevin understood the man did more than expect him to say yes; to Pop it was inconceivable that he could say no. Kevin thought, *If I said no he wouldn't hear it; he'd say "Good, that's agreed, then," and I'd end up back on the sidewalk with his money in my pocket whether I wanted it or not.*

And he *did* have his birthday money.

All the same, there was that chill wind to think about. That wind that seemed to blow not from the surface but right out of those photographs in spite of their deceptively flat, deceptively shiny surfaces. He felt that wind coming from them despite their mute declaration which averred *We are Polaroids, and for no reason we can tell or even understand, we show only the undramatic surfaces of things.* That wind was there. What about that wind?

Kevin hesitated a moment longer and the bright eyes behind the rimless spectacles measured him. *I ain't gonna ask you if you're a man or a mouse,* Pop Merrill's eyes said. *You're fifteen years old, and what I mean to say is at fifteen you may not be a*

man yet, not quite, but you are too goddam old to be a mouse and both
of us know it. And besides you're not from Away; you're from town,
just like me.

"Sure," Kevin said with a hollow lightness in his voice. It
fooled neither of them. "I can get the film tonight, I guess, and
bring the pictures in tomorrow, after school."

"Nope," Pop said.

"You're closed tomorrow?"

"Nope," Pop said, and because he *was* from town, Kevin
waited patiently. "You're thinkin about takin thirty pitchers
all at once, aren't you?"

"I guess so."

"That ain't the way I want you to do it," Pop said. "It don't
matter *where* you take them, but it *does* matter *when.* Here.
Lemme figure."

Pop figured, and then even wrote down a list of times,
which Kevin pocketed.

"So!" Pop said, rubbing his hands briskly together so that
they made a dry sound that was like two pieces of used-up
sandpaper rubbing together. "You'll see me in . . . oh, three
days or so?"

"Yes . . . I guess so."

"I'll bet you'd just as lief wait until Monday after school,
anyway," Pop said. He dropped Kevin a fourth wink, slow and
sly and humiliating in the extreme. "So your friends don't see
you coming in here and tax you with it, is what I mean to say."

Kevin flushed and dropped his eyes to the worktable and
began to gather up the Polaroids so his hands would have
something to do. When he was embarrassed and they didn't,
he cracked his knuckles.

"I—" He began some sort of absurd protest that would con-
vince neither of them and then stopped, staring down at one
of the photos.

"What?" Pop asked. For the first time since Kevin had
approached him, Pop sounded entirely human, but Kevin

hardly heard his words, much less his tone of faint alarm. "Now you look like *you* seen a ghost, boy."

"No," Kevin said. "No ghost. I see who took the picture. Who *really* took the picture."

"What in glory are you talking about?"

Kevin pointed to a shadow. He, his father, his mother, Meg, and apparently Mr. Merrill himself had taken it for the shadow of a tree that wasn't itself in the frame. But it wasn't a tree. Kevin saw that now, and what you had seen could never be unseen.

More hieroglyphics on the plinth.

"I don't see what you're gettin at," Pop said. But Kevin knew the old man knew he was getting at *something,* which was why he sounded put out.

"Look at the shadow of the dog first," Kevin said. "Then look at this one here again." He tapped the left side of the photograph. "In the picture, the sun is either going down or coming up. That makes all the shadows long, and it's hard to tell what's throwing them. But looking at it, just now, it clicked home for me."

"*What* clicked home, son?" Pop reached for the drawer, probably meaning to get the magnifying glass with the light in it again . . . and then stopped. All at once he didn't need it. All at once it had clicked into place for him, too.

"It's the shadow of a man, ain't it?" Pop said. "I be go to hell if that one ain't the shadow of a man."

"Or a woman. You can't tell. Those are legs, I'm sure they are, but they could belong to a woman wearing pants. Or even a kid. With the shadow running so long—"

"Ayuh, you can't tell."

Kevin said, "It's the shadow of whoever took it, isn't it?"

"Ayuh."

"But it wasn't *me,*" Kevin said. "It came out of my camera— all of them did—but I didn't take it. So who did, Mr. Merrill? Who did?"

"Call me Pop," the old man said absently, looking at the shadow in the picture, and Kevin felt his chest swell with pleasure as those few clocks still capable of running a little fast began to signal the others that, weary as they might be, it was time to charge the half-hour.

CHAPTER THREE

When Kevin arrived back at the Emporium Galorium with the photographs on Monday after school, the leaves had begun to turn color. He had been fifteen for almost two weeks and the novelty had worn off.

The novelty of that plinth, *the supernatural,* had not, but this wasn't anything he counted among his blessings. He had finished taking the schedule of photographs Pop had given him, and by the time he had, he had seen clearly—clearly enough, anyway—why Pop had wanted him to take them at intervals: the first ten on the hour, then let the camera rest, the second ten every two hours, and the third at three-hour intervals. He'd taken the last few that day at school. He had seen something else as well, something none of them *could* have seen at first; it was not clearly visible until the final three pictures. They had scared him so badly he had decided, even before taking the pictures to the Emporium Galorium, that he wanted to get rid of the Sun 660. Not exchange it; that was the last thing he wanted to do, because it would mean the camera would be out of his hands and hence out of his control. He couldn't have that.

It's mine, he had thought, and the thought kept recurring, but it wasn't a *true* thought. If it was—if the Sun only took pictures of the black breedless dog by the white picket fence when he, Kevin, was the one pushing the trigger—that would have been one thing. But that wasn't the case. Whatever the nasty magic inside the Sun might be, he was not its sole initiator. His father had taken the same (well, *almost* the same) picture, and so had Pop Merrill, and so had Meg when Kevin had

36

let her take a couple of the pictures on Pop's carefully timed schedule.

"Did you number em, like I asked?" Pop asked when Kevin delivered them.

"Yes, one to fifty-eight," Kevin said. He thumbed through the stack of photographs, showing Pop the small circled numbers in the lower lefthand corner of each. "But I don't know if it matters. I've decided to get rid of the camera."

"Get rid of it? That ain't what you mean."

"No. I guess not. I'm going to break it up with a sledge-hammer."

Pop looked at him with those shrewd little eyes. "That so?"

"Yes," Kevin said, meeting the shrewd gaze steadfastly. "Last week I would have laughed at the idea, but I'm not laughing now. I think the thing is dangerous."

"Well, I guess you could be right, and I guess you could tape a charge of dynamite to it and blow it to smithereens if you wanted. It's yours, is what I mean to say. But why don't you hold off a little while? There's somethin I want to do with these pitchers. You might be interested."

"What?"

"I druther not say," Pop answered, "case it don't turn out. But I might have somethin by the end of the week that'd help you decide better, one way or the other."

"I *have* decided," Kevin said, and tapped something that had shown up in the last two photographs.

"What *is* it?" Pop asked. "I've looked at it with m'glass, and I feel like I *should* know what it is—it's like a name you can't quite remember but have right on the tip of your tongue, is what I mean to say—but I don't quite."

"I suppose I could hold off until Friday or so," Kevin said, choosing not to answer the old man's question. "I really don't want to hold off much longer."

"Scared?"

"Yes," Kevin said simply. "I'm scared."

"You told your folks?"

"Not all of it, no."

"Well, you might want to. Might want to tell your dad, anyway, is what I mean to say. You got time to think on it while I take care of what it is I want to take care of."

"No matter what you want to do, I'm going to put my dad's sledgehammer on it come Friday," Kevin said. "I don't even *want* a camera anymore. Not a Polaroid or any other kind."

"Where is it now?"

"In my bureau drawer. And that's where it's going to stay."

"Stop by the store here on Friday," Pop said. "Bring the camera with you. We'll take a look at this little idear of mine, and then, if you want to bust the goddam thing up, I'll provide the sledgehammer myself. No charge. Even got a chopping block out back you can set it on."

"That's a deal," Kevin said, and smiled.

"Just what *have* you told your folks about all this?"

"That I'm still deciding. I didn't want to worry them. My mom, especially." Kevin looked at him curiously. "Why did you say I might want to tell my dad?"

"You bust up that camera, your father is going to be mad at you," Pop said. "That ain't so bad, but he's maybe gonna think you're a little bit of a fool, too. Or an old maid, squallin burglar to the police on account of a creaky board, is what I mean to say."

Kevin flushed a little, thinking of how angry his father had gotten when the idea of the supernatural had come up, then sighed. He hadn't thought of it in that light at all, but now that he did, he thought Pop was probably right. He didn't like the idea of his father being mad at him, but he could live with it. The idea that his father might think him a coward, a fool, or both, though . . . that was a different kettle of fish altogether.

Pop was watching him shrewdly, reading these thoughts as they crossed Kevin's face as easily as a man might read the headlines on the front page of a tabloid newspaper.

"You think he could meet you here around four in the afternoon on Friday?"

"No way," Kevin said. "He works in Portland. He hardly ever gets home before six."

"I'll give him a call, if you want," Pop said. "He'll come if I call."

Kevin gave him a wide-eyed stare.

Pop smiled thinly. "Oh, I know him," he said. "Know him of old. He don't like to let on about me any more than you do, and I understand that, but what I mean to say is I know him. I know a lot of people in this town. You'd be surprised, son."

"How?"

"Did him a favor one time," Pop said. He popped a match alight with his thumbnail, and veiled those eyes behind enough smoke so you couldn't tell if it was amusement, sentiment, or contempt in them.

"What kind of favor?"

"That," Pop said, "is between him and me. Just like this business here"—he gestured at the pile of photographs—"is between me and you. *That's* what I mean to say."

"Well . . . okay . . . I guess. Should I say anything to him?"

"Nope!" Pop said in his chipper way. "You let me take care of everything." And for a moment, in spite of the obfuscating pipe-smoke, there was something in Pop Merrill's eyes Kevin Delevan didn't care for. He went out, a sorely confused boy who knew only one thing for sure: he wanted this to be over.

When he was gone, Pop sat silent and moveless for nearly five minutes. He allowed his pipe to go out in his mouth and drummed his fingers, which were nearly as knowing and talented as those of a concert violinist but masqueraded as equipment which should more properly have belonged to a digger of ditches or a pourer of cement, next to the stack of photographs. As the smoke dissipated, his eyes stood out clearly, and they were as cold as ice in a December puddle.

Abruptly he put the pipe in its holder and called a camera-and-video shop in Lewiston. He asked two questions. The answer to both of them was yes. Pop hung up the phone and went back to drumming his fingers on the table beside the Polaroids. What he was planning wasn't really fair to the boy, but the boy had uncovered the corner of something he not only didn't understand but didn't *want* to understand.

Fair or not, Pop didn't believe he intended to let the boy do what the boy wanted to do. He hadn't decided what he himself meant to do, not yet, not entirely, but it was wise to be prepared.

That was *always* wise.

. He sat and drummed his fingers and wondered what that thing was the boy had seen. He had obviously felt Pop would know—or might know—but Pop hadn't a clue. The boy might tell him on Friday. Or not. But if the boy didn't, the father, to whom Pop had once loaned four hundred dollars to cover a bet on a basketball game, a bet he had lost and which his wife knew nothing about, certainly would. If, that was, he could. Even the best of fathers didn't know all about their sons anymore once those sons were fifteen or so, but Pop thought Kevin was a very *young* fifteen, and that his dad knew most things . . . or could find them out.

He smiled and drummed his fingers and all the clocks began to charge wearily at the hour of five.

CHAPTER FOUR

Pop Merrill turned the sign which hung in his door from OPEN to CLOSED at two o'clock on Friday afternoon, slipped himself behind the wheel of his 1959 Chevrolet, which had been for years perfectly maintained at Sonny's Texaco at absolutely no cost at all (the fallout of another little loan, and Sonny Jackett another town fellow who would prefer hot coals pressed against the soles of his feet to admitting that he not only knew but was deeply indebted to Pop Merrill, who had gotten him out of a desperate scrape over in New Hampshire in '69), and took himself up to Lewiston, a city he hated because it seemed to him that there were only two streets in the whole town (maybe three) that weren't one-ways. He arrived as he always did when Lewiston and only Lewiston would do: not by driving to it but arriving somewhere near it and then spiraling slowly inward along those beshitted one-way streets until he reckoned he was as close as he could get and then walking the rest of the way, a tall thin man with a bald head, rimless specs, clean khaki pants with creases and cuffs, and a blue workman's shirt buttoned right up to the collar.

There was a sign in the window of Twin City Camera and Video that showed a cartoon man who appeared to be battling a huge tangle of movie-film and losing. The fellow looked just about ready to blow his stack. The words over and under the picture read: TIRED OF FIGHTING? WE TRANSFER YOUR 8 MM MOVIES (SNAPSHOTS TOO!) ONTO VIDEO TAPE!

Just another goddam gadget, Pop thought, opening the door and going in. World's dying of em.

But he was one of those people—world's dying of em—not

at all above using what he disparaged if it proved expedient. He spoke briefly with the clerk. The clerk got the proprietor. They had known each other for many years (probably since Homer sailed the wine-dark sea, some wits might have said). The proprietor invited Pop into the back room, where they shared a nip.

"That's a goddam strange bunch of photos," the proprietor said.

"Ayuh."

"The videotape I made of them is even stranger."

"I bet so."

"That all you got to say?"

"Ayuh."

"Fuck ya, then," the proprietor said, and they both cackled their shrill old-man's cackles. Behind the counter, the clerk winced.

Pop left twenty minutes later with two items: a video cassette, and a brand-new Polaroid Sun 660, still in its box.

When he got back to the shop, he called Kevin's house. He was not surprised when it was John Delevan who answered.

"If you've been fucking my boy over, I'll kill you, you old snake," John Delevan said without preamble, and distantly Pop could hear the boy's wounded cry: *"Da-ad!"*

Pop's lips skinned back from his teeth—crooked, eroded, pipe-yellow, but his own, by the bald-headed Christ—and if Kevin had seen him in that moment he would have done more than *wonder* if maybe Pop Merrill was something other than the Castle Rock version of the Kindly Old Sage of the Cracker-barrel: he would have *known*.

"Now, John," he said. "I've been trying to *help* your boy with that camera. That's all in the world I've been trying to do." He paused. "Just like that one time I gave you a help when you got a little too proud of the Seventy-Sixers, is what I mean to say."

A thundering silence from John Delevan's end of the line which meant he had plenty to say on *that* subject, but the kiddo was in the room and that was as good as a gag.

"Now, your kid don't know nothing about *that,*" Pop said, that nasty grin broadening in the tick-tock shadows of the Emporium Galorium, where the dominant smells were old magazines and mouse-turds. "I told him it wasn't none of his business, just like I told him that this business here *was.* I wouldn't have even brought up that bet if I knew another way to get you here, is what I mean to say. And you ought to see what I've got, John, because if you don't you won't understand why the boy wants to smash that camera you bought him—"

"*Smash* it!"

"—and why I think it's a hell of a good idea. Now are you going to come down here with him, or not?"

"I'm not in Portland, am I, dammit?"

"Never mind the CLOSED sign on the door," Pop said in the serene tone of a man who has been getting his own way for many years and expects to go right on getting it for many more. "Just knock."

"Who in hell gave my boy your name, Merrill?"

"I didn't ask him," Pop said in that same infuriatingly serene tone of voice, and hung up the telephone. And, to the empty shop: "All I know is that he came. Just like they always do."

While he waited, he took the Sun 660 he had bought in Lewiston out of its box and buried the box deep in the trash-can beside his worktable. He looked at the camera thoughtfully, then loaded the four-picture starter-pack that came with the camera. With that done, he unfolded the body of the camera, exposing the lens. The red light to the left of the lightning-bolt shape came on briefly, and then the green one began to stutter. Pop was not very surprised to find he was filled with trepidation. *Well,* he thought, *God hates a coward,* and pushed the shutter-release. The clutter of the Emporium Galorium's barnlike interior was bathed in an instant of merciless and improbable white light. The camera made its squidgy little whine and spat out what would be a Polaroid picture— perfectly adequate but somehow lacking; a picture that was all surfaces depicting a world where ships undoubtedly *would* sail off the fuming and monster-raddled edge of the earth if they went far enough west.

Pop watched it with the same mesmerized expression Clan Delevan had worn as it waited for Kevin's first picture to develop. He told himself this camera would not do the same thing, of course not, but he was stiff and wiry with tension just the same and, tough old bird or not, if a random board had creaked in the place just then, he almost certainly would have cried out.

But no board *did* creak, and when the picture developed it showed only what it was supposed to show: clocks assembled, clocks in pieces, toasters, stacks of magazines tied with twine, lamps with shades so horrible only women of the British upper classes could truly love them, shelves of quarter paperbacks (six for a buck) with titles like *After Dark My Sweet* and *Fire in the Flesh* and *The Brass Cupcake,* and, in the distant background, the dusty front window. You could read the letters EMPOR backward before the bulky silhouette of a bureau blocked off the rest.

No hulking creature from beyond the grave; no knife-wielding doll in blue overalls. Just a camera. He supposed the whim which had caused him to take a picture in the first place, just to see, showed how deeply this thing had worked its way under his skin.

Pop sighed and buried the photograph in the trash-can. He opened the wide drawer of the worktable and took out a small hammer. He held the camera firmly in his left hand and then swung the hammer on a short arc through the dusty tick-tock air. He didn't use a great deal of force. There was no need. Nobody took any pride in workmanship anymore. They talked about the wonders of modern science, synthetics, new alloys, polymers, Christ knew what. It didn't matter. Snot. That was what everything was *really* made out of these days, and you didn't have to work very hard to bust a camera that was made of snot.

The lens shattered. Shards of plastic flew from around it, and that reminded Pop of something else. Had it been the left or right side? He frowned. Left. He thought. They wouldn't notice anyway, or remember which side themselves if they did, you could damn near take that to the bank, but Pop hadn't feathered his nest with damn-nears. It was wise to be prepared.

Always wise.

He replaced the hammer, used a small brush to sweep the broken chunks of glass and plastic off the table and onto the floor, then returned the brush and took out a grease-pencil with a fine tip and an X-Act-O knife. He drew what he thought was the approximate shape of the piece of plastic which had broken off Kevin Delevan's Sun when Meg knocked it on the floor, then used the X-Act-O to carve along the lines. When he thought he had dug deep enough into the plastic, he put the X-Act-O back in the drawer, and then knocked the Polaroid camera off the worktable. What had happened once ought to happen again, especially with the fault-lines he had pre-carved.

It worked pretty slick, too. He examined the camera, which now had a chunk of plastic gone from the side as well as a busted lens, nodded, and placed it in the deep shadow under the worktable. Then he found the piece of plastic that had split off from the camera, and buried it in the trash along with the box and the single exposure he had taken.

Now there was nothing to do but wait for the Delevans to arrive. Pop took the video cassette upstairs to the cramped little apartment where he lived. He put it on top of the VCR he had bought to watch the fuck-movies you could buy now-adays, then sat down to read the paper. He saw there had been a plane-crash in Pakistan. A hundred and thirty people killed. Goddam fools were always getting themselves killed, Pop thought, but that was all right. A few less woggies in the world was a good thing all around. Then he turned to the sports to see how the Red Sox had done. They still had a good chance of winning the Eastern Division.

CHAPTER FIVE

"What was it?" Kevin asked as they prepared to go. They had the house to themselves. Meg was at her ballet class, and it was Mrs. Delevan's day to play bridge with her friends. She would come home at five with a large loaded pizza and news of who was getting divorced or at least thinking of it.

"None of your business," Mr. Delevan said in a rough voice which was both angry and embarrassed.

The day was chilly. Mr. Delevan had been looking for his light jacket. Now he stopped and turned around and looked at his son, who was standing behind him, wearing his own jacket and holding the Sun camera in one hand.

"All right," he said. "I never pulled that crap on you before and I guess I don't want to start now. You know what I mean."

"Yes," Kevin said, and thought: *I know exactly what you're talking about, is what I mean to say.*

"Your mother doesn't know anything about this."

"I won't tell her."

"Don't say that," his father told him sharply. "Don't start down that road or you'll never stop."

"But you said you never—"

"No, I never told her," his father said, finding the jacket at last and shrugging into it. "She never asked and I never told her. If she never asks you, you never have to tell her. That sound like a bullshit qualification to you?"

"Yeah," Kevin said. "To tell the truth, it does."

"Okay," Mr. Delevan said. "Okay . . . but that's the way we do it. If the subject ever comes up, you—*we*—have to tell. If it doesn't, we don't. That's just the way we do things in the

47

grown-up world. It sounds fucked up, I guess, and sometimes it is fucked up, but that's how we do it. Can you live with that?"

"Yes. I guess so."

"Good. Let's go."

They walked down the driveway side by side, zipping their jackets. The wind played with the hair at John Delevan's temples, and Kevin noted for the first time—with uneasy surprise—that his father was starting to go gray there.

"It was no big deal, anyway," Mr. Delevan said. He might almost have been talking to himself. "It never is with Pop Merrill. He isn't a big-deal kind of guy, if you know what I mean."

Kevin nodded.

"He's a fairly wealthy man, you know, but that junk-shop of his isn't the reason why. He's Castle Rock's version of Shylock."

"Of who?"

"Never mind. You'll read the play sooner or later if education hasn't gone entirely to hell. He loans money at interest rates that are higher than the law allows."

"Why would people borrow from him?" Kevin asked as they walked toward downtown under trees from which leaves of red and purple and gold sifted slowly down.

"Because," Mr. Delevan said sourly, "they can't borrow anyplace else."

"You mean their credit's no good?"

"Something like that."

"But we . . . you . . ."

"Yeah. We're doing all right now. But we weren't *always* doing all right. When your mother and I were first married, how we were doing was all the way across town from all right."

He fell silent again for a time, and Kevin didn't interrupt him.

"Well, there was a guy who was awful proud of the Celtics one year," his father said. He was looking down at his feet, as if afraid to step on a crack and break his mother's back. "They were going into the play-offs against the Philadelphia Seventy-Sixers. They—the Celtics—were favored to win, but by a lot less than usual. I had a feeling the Seventy-Sixers were going to take them, that it was their year."

He looked quickly at his son, almost snatching the glance as a shoplifter might take a small but fairly valuable item and tuck it into his coat, and then went back to minding the cracks in the sidewalk again. They were now walking down Castle Hill and toward the town's single signal-light at the crossing of Lower Main Street and Watermill Lane. Beyond the intersection, what locals called the Tin Bridge crossed Castle Stream. Its overstructure cut the deep-blue autumn sky into neat geometrical shapes.

"I guess it's that feeling, that special *sureness,* that infects the poor souls who lose their bank accounts, their houses, their cars, even the clothes they stand up in at casinos and back-room poker games. That feeling that you got a telegram from God. I only got it that once, and I thank God for that.

"In those days I'd make a friendly bet on a football game or the World Series with somebody, five dollars was the most, I think, and usually it was a lot less than that, just a token thing, a quarter or maybe a pack of cigarettes."

This time it was Kevin who shoplifted a glance, only Mr. Delevan caught it, cracks in the sidewalk or no cracks.

"Yes, I smoked in those days, too. Now I don't smoke and I don't bet. Not since that last one. That last one cured me.

"Back then your mother and I had only been married two years. You weren't born yet. I was working as a surveyor's assistant, bringing home just about a hundred and sixteen dollars a week. Or that was what I cleared, anyway, when the government finally let go of it.

"This fellow who was so proud of the Celtics was one of the engineers. He even wore one of those green Celtics warm-up jackets to work, the kind that have the shamrock on the back.

The week before the play-offs, he kept saying he'd like to find someone brave enough and stupid enough to bet on the Seventy-Sixers, because he had four hundred dollars just waiting to catch him a dividend.

"That voice inside me kept getting louder and louder, and the day before the championship series started, I went up to him on lunch-break. My heart felt like it was going to tear right out of my chest, I was so scared."

"Because you didn't have four hundred dollars," Kevin said. "The other guy did, but you didn't." He was looking at his father openly now, the camera completely forgotten for the first time since his first visit to Pop Merrill. The wonder of what the Sun 660 was doing was lost—temporarily, anyway—in this newer, brighter wonder: as a young man his father had done something spectacularly stupid, just as Kevin knew other men did, just as he might do himself someday, when he was on his own and there was no adult member of the Reasonable tribe to protect him from some terrible impulse, some misbegotten instinct. His father, it seemed, had briefly been a member of the Instinctive tribe himself. It was hard to believe, but wasn't this the proof?

"Right."

"But you bet him."

"Not right away," his father said. "I told him I thought the Seventy-Sixers would take the championship, but four hundred bucks was a lot to risk for a guy who was only a surveyor's assistant."

"But you never came right out and told him you didn't have the money."

"I'm afraid it went a little further than that, Kevin. I implied I *did* have it. I said I couldn't afford to *lose* four hundred dollars, and that was disingenuous, to say the least. I told him I couldn't risk that kind of money on an even bet—still not lying, you see, but skating right up to the edge of the lie. *Do* you see?"

"Yes."

"I don't know what would have happened—maybe nothing—
if the foreman hadn't rung the back-to-work bell right then.
But he did, and this engineer threw up his hands and said, 'I'll
give you two-to-one, sonny, if that's what you want. It don't
matter to me. It's still gonna be four hundred in my pocket.'
And before I knew what was happening we'd shook on it with
half a dozen men watching and I was in the soup, for better or
worse. And going home that night I thought of your mother,
and what she'd say if she knew, and I pulled over to the shoulder of the road in the old Ford I had back then and I puked out
the door."

A police car came rolling slowly down Harrington Street.
Norris Ridgewick was driving and Andy Clutterbuck was rid-
ing shotgun. Clut raised his hand as the cruiser turned left
on Main Street. John and Kevin Delevan raised their hands
in return, and autumn drowsed peacefully around them as if
John Delevan had never sat in the open door of his old Ford
and puked into the road-dust between his own feet.

They crossed Main Street.

"Well . . . you could say I got my money's worth, anyway.
The Sixers took it right to the last few seconds of the seventh
game, and then one of those Irish bastards—I forget which
one it was—stole the ball from Hal Greer and went to the hole
with it and there went the four hundred dollars I didn't have.
When I paid that goddam engineer off the next day he said he
'got a little nervous there near the end.' That was all. I could
have popped his eyes out with my thumbs."

"You paid him off the next *day*? How'd you do that?"

"I told you, it was like a fever. Once we shook hands on the
bet, the fever passed. I hoped like hell I'd win that bet, but
I knew I'd have to *think* like I was going to lose. There was a
lot more at stake than just four hundred dollars. There was
the question of my job, of course, and what might happen if I
wasn't able to pay off the guy I'd bet with. He was an engineer,

after all, and technically my boss. That fellow had just enough son of a bitch in him to have fired my ass if I didn't pay the wager. It wouldn't have been the bet, but he would have found something, and it would have been something that would go on my work-record in big red letters, too. But that wasn't the biggest thing. Not at all."

"What was?"

"Your mother. Our marriage. When you're young and don't have either a pot to piss in or a window to throw it out of, a marriage is under strain all the time. It doesn't matter how much you love each other, that marriage is like an overloaded packhorse and you know it can fall to its knees or even roll over dead if all the wrong things happen at all the wrong times. I don't think she would have divorced me over a four-hundred-dollar bet, but I'm glad I never had to find out for sure. So when the fever passed, I saw that I might have bet a little more than four hundred dollars. I might just have bet my whole goddam future."

They were approaching the Emporium Galorium. There was a bench on the verge of the grassy town common, and Mr. Delevan gestured for Kevin to sit down.

"This won't take long," he said, and then laughed. It was a grating, compressed sound, like an inexperienced driver working a transmission lever. "It hurts too much to stretch out, even after all these years."

So they sat on the bench and Mr. Delevan finished the story of how he happened to know Pop Merrill while they looked across the grassy common with the bandstand in the middle.

"I went to him the same night I made the bet," he said. "I told your mother I was going out for cigarettes. I went after dark, so no one would see me. From town, I mean. They would have known I was in some kind of trouble, and I didn't want that. I went in and Pop said, 'What's a professional man like you doing in a place like this, Mr. John Delevan?' and I told him what I'd done and he said, 'You made a bet and already you have got your head set to the idea you've lost it.' 'If I do lose it,' I said, 'I want to make sure I don't lose anything else.'

"That made him laugh. 'I respect a wise man,' he said. 'I reckon I can trust you. If the Celtics win, you come see me. I'll take care of you. You got an honest face.'"

"And that was *all?*" Kevin asked. In eighth-grade math, they had done a unit on loans, and he still remembered most of it. "He didn't ask for any, uh, collateral?"

"People who go to Pop don't have collateral," his father said. "He's not a loan-shark like you see in the movies; he doesn't break any legs if you don't pay up. But he has ways of fixing people."

"What ways?"

"Never mind," John Delevan said. "After that last game ended, I went upstairs to tell your mother I was going to go out for cigarettes—again. She was asleep, though, so I was spared that lie. It was late, late for Castle Rock, anyway, going on eleven, but the lights were on in his place. I knew they would be. He gave me the money in tens. He took them out of an old Crisco can. All tens. I remember that. They were crumpled but he had made them straight. Forty ten-dollar bills, him counting them out like a bank-clerk with that pipe going and his glasses up on his head and for just a second there I felt like knocking his teeth out. Instead I thanked him. You don't know how hard it can be to say thank you sometimes. I hope you never do. He said, 'You understand the terms, now, don't you?' and I said I did, and he said, 'That's good. I ain't worried about you. What I mean to say is you got an honest face. You go on and take care of your business with that fella at work, and then take care of your business with me. And don't make any more bets. Man only has to look in your face to see you weren't cut out to be a gambler.' So I took the money and went home and put it under the floor-mat of the old Chevy and lay next to your mother and didn't sleep a wink all night long because I felt filthy. Next day I gave the tens to the engineer

I bet with, and *he* counted them out, and then he just folded them over and tucked them into one of his shirt pockets and buttoned the flap like that cash didn't mean any more than a gas receipt he'd have to turn in to the chief contractor at the end of the day. Then he clapped me on the shoulder and said, 'Well, you're a good man, Johnny. Better than I thought. I won four hundred but I lost twenty to Bill Untermeyer. He bet you'd come up with the dough first thing this morning and I bet him I wouldn't see it till the end of the week. If I ever did.' 'I pay my debts,' I said. 'Easy, now,' he said, and clapped me on the shoulder again, and I think that time I really *did* come close to popping his eyeballs out with my thumbs."

"How much interest did Pop charge you, Dad?"

His father looked at him sharply. "Does he let you call him that?"

"Yeah, why?"

"Watch out for him, then," Mr. Delevan said. "He's a snake."

Then he sighed, as if admitting to both of them that he was begging the question, and knew it. "Ten per cent. That's what the interest was."

"That's not so m—"

"Compounded weekly," Mr. Delevan added.

Kevin sat struck dumb for a moment. Then: "But that's not *legal!*"

"How true," Mr. Delevan said dryly. He looked at the strained expression of incredulity on his son's face and his own strained look broke. He laughed and clapped his son on the shoulder. "It's only the world, Kev," he said. "It kills us all in the end, anyhow."

"But—"

"But nothing. That was the freight, and he knew I'd pay it. I knew they were hiring on the three-to-eleven shift at the mill over in Oxford. I told you I'd gotten myself ready to lose, and going to Pop wasn't the only thing I did. I'd talked to your mother, said I might take a shift over there for awhile. After all, she'd been wanting a newer car, and maybe to move to a better apartment, and get a little something into the bank in case we had some kind of financial setback."

He laughed.

"Well, the financial setback had happened, and she didn't know it, and I meant to do my damnedest to keep her from finding out. I didn't know if I could or not, but I meant to do my damnedest. She was dead set against it. She said I'd kill myself, working sixteen hours a day. She said those mills were dangerous, you were always reading about someone losing an arm or leg or even getting crushed to death under the rollers. I told her not to worry, I'd get a job in the sorting room, minimum wage but sit-down work, and if it really *was* too much, I'd give it up. She was still against it. She said she'd go to work herself, but I talked her out of *that*. That was the last thing I wanted, you know."

Kevin nodded.

"I told her I'd quit six months, eight at the outside, anyway. So I went up and they hired me on, but not in the sorting room. I got a job in the rolling shed, feeding raw stock into a machine that looked like the wringer on a giant's washing machine. It was dangerous work, all right; if you slipped or if your attention wandered—and it was hard to keep that from happening because it was so damned monotonous—you'd lose part of yourself or all of it. I saw a man lose his hand in a roller once and I never want to see anything like that again. It was like watching a charge of dynamite go off in a rubber glove stuffed with meat."

"God-*damn,*" Kevin said. He had rarely said that in his father's presence, but his father did not seem to notice.

"Anyway, I got two dollars and eighty cents an hour, and after two months they bumped me to three ten," he said. "It was hell. I'd work on the road project all day long—at least it was early spring and not hot—and then race off to the mill, pushing that Chevy for all it was worth to keep from being late. I'd take off my khakis and just about jump into a pair of blue-jeans and a tee-shirt and work the rollers from three until eleven. I'd get home around midnight and the worst part was the nights when your mother waited up—which she did two or three nights a week—and I'd have to act cheery and full of pep when I could hardly walk a straight line, I was so tired. But if she'd seen that—"

"She would have made you stop."

"Yes. She would. So I'd act bright and chipper and tell her funny stories about the sorting room where I wasn't working and sometimes I'd wonder what would happen if she ever decided to drive up some night—to give me a hot dinner, or something like that. I did a pretty good job, but some of it must have showed, because she kept telling me I was silly to be knocking myself out for so little—and it really *did* seem like chicken-feed once the government dipped their beak and Pop dipped his. It seemed like just about what a fellow working in the sorting room for minimum wage would clear. They paid Wednesday afternoons, and I always made sure to cash my check in the office before the girls went home.

"Your mother never saw one of those checks.

"The first week I paid Pop fifty dollars—forty was interest, and ten was on the four hundred, which left three hundred and ninety owing. I was like a walking zombie. On the road I'd sit in my car at lunch, eat my sandwich, and then sleep until the foreman rang his goddamned bell. I *hated* that bell.

"I paid him fifty dollars the second week—thirty-nine was interest, eleven was on the principal—and I had it down to three hundred and seventy-nine dollars. I felt like a bird trying to eat a mountain one peck at a time.

"The third week I almost went into the roller myself, and it scared me so bad I woke up for a few minutes—enough to have an idea, anyway, so I guess it was a blessing in disguise. I had to give up smoking. I couldn't understand why I hadn't seen it before. In those days a pack of smokes cost forty cents.

I smoked two packs a day. That was five dollars and sixty cents a week!

"We had a cigarette break every two hours and I looked at my pack of Tareytons and saw I had ten, maybe twelve. I made those cigarettes last a week and a half, and I never bought another pack.

"I spent a month not knowing if I could make it or not. There were days when the alarm went off at six o'clock and I knew I couldn't, that I'd just have to tell Mary and take whatever she wanted to dish out. But by the time the second month started, I knew I was probably going to be all right. I think to this day it was the extra five sixty a week—that, and all the returnable beer and soda bottles I could pick up along the sides of the road—that made the difference. I had the principal down to three hundred, and that meant I could knock off twenty-five, twenty-six dollars a week from it, more as time went on.

"Then, in late April, we finished the road project and got a week off, with pay. I told Mary I was getting ready to quit my job at the mill and she said thank God, and I spent that week off from my regular job working all the hours I could get at the mill, because it was time and a half. I never had an accident. I saw them, saw men fresher and more awake than I was have them, but I never did. I don't know why. At the end of that week I gave Pop Merrill a hundred dollars and gave my week's notice at the paper mill. After that last week I had whittled the nut down enough so I could chip the rest off my regular pay-check without your mother noticing."

He fetched a deep sigh.

"Now you know how I know Pop Merrill, and why I don't trust him. I spent ten weeks in hell and he reaped the sweat off my forehead and my ass, too, in ten-dollar bills that he undoubtedly took out of that Crisco can or another one and passed on to some other sad sack who had got himself in the same kind of mess I did."

"Boy, you must hate him."

"No," Mr. Delevan said, getting up. "I don't hate him and I don't hate myself. I got a fever, that's all. It could have been worse. My marriage could have died of it, and you and Meg never would have been born, Kevin. Or I might have died of it myself. Pop Merrill was the cure. He was a *hard* cure, but he worked. What's hard to forgive is *how* he worked. He took every damned cent and wrote it down in a book in a drawer under his cash register and looked at the circles under my eyes and the way my pants had gotten a way of hanging off my hipbones and he said nothing."

They walked toward the Emporium Galorium, which was painted the dusty faded yellow of signs left too long in country store windows, its false front both obvious and unapologetic. Next to it, Polly Chalmers was sweeping her walk and talking to Alan Pangborn, the county sheriff. She looked young and fresh with her hair pulled back in a horsetail; he looked young and heroic in his neatly pressed uniform. But things were not always the way they looked; even Kevin, at fifteen, knew that. Sheriff Pangborn had lost his wife and youngest son in a car accident that spring, and Kevin had heard that Ms. Chalmers, young or not, had a bad case of arthritis and might be crippled up with it before too many more years passed. Things were not always the way they looked. This thought caused him to glance toward the Emporium Galorium again . . . and then to look down at his birthday camera, which he was carrying in his hand.

"He even did me a favor," Mr. Delevan mused. "He got me to quit smoking. But I don't trust him. Walk careful around him, Kevin. And no matter what, let me do the talking. I might know him a little better now."

So they went into the dusty ticking silence, where Pop Merrill waited for them by the door, with his glasses propped on the bald dome of his head and a trick or two still up his sleeve.

CHAPTER SIX

"Well, and here you are, father and son," Pop said, giving them an admiring, grandfatherly smile. His eyes twinkled behind a haze of pipe-smoke and for a moment, although he was clean-shaven, Kevin thought Pop looked like Father Christmas. "You've got a fine boy, Mr. Delevan. *Fine.*"

"I know," Mr. Delevan said. "I was upset when I heard he'd been dealing with you because I want him to stay that way."

"That's hard," Pop said, with the faintest touch of reproach. "That's hard comin from a man who when he had nowhere else to turn—"

"That's over," Mr. Delevan said.

"Ayuh, ayuh, that's just what I mean to say."

"But this isn't."

"It will be," Pop said. He held a hand out to Kevin and Kevin gave him the Sun camera. "It will be today." He held the camera up, turning it over in his hands. "This is a piece of work. What *kind* of piece I don't know, but your boy wants to smash it because he thinks it's dangerous. I think he's right. But I told him, 'You don't want your daddy to think you're a sissy, do you?' That's the only reason I had him ho you down here, John—"

"I liked 'Mr. Delevan' better."

"All right," Pop said, and sighed. "I can see you ain't gonna warm up none and let bygones be bygones."

"No."

Kevin looked from one man to the other, his face distressed.

"Well, it don't matter," Pop said; both his voice and face

went cold with remarkable suddenness, and he didn't look like Father Christmas at all. "When I said the past is the past and what's done is done, I meant it . . . except when it affects what people do in the here and now. But I'm gonna say this, Mr. Delevan: I don't bottom deal, and you know it."

Pop delivered this magnificent lie with such flat coldness that both of them believed it; Mr. Delevan even felt a little ashamed of himself, as incredible as that was.

"Our business was our business. You told me what you wanted, I told you what I'd have to have in return, and you give it to me, and there was an end to it. This is another thing." And then Pop told a lie even more magnificent, a lie which was simply too towering to be disbelieved. "I got no stake in this, Mr. Delevan. There is nothing I want but to help your boy. I like him."

He smiled and Father Christmas was back so fast and strong that Kevin forgot he had ever been gone. Yet more than this: John Delevan, who had for months worked himself to the edge of exhaustion and perhaps even death between the rollers in order to pay the exorbitant price this man demanded to atone for a momentary lapse into insanity—John Delevan forgot that other expression, too.

Pop led them along the twisting aisles, through the smell of dead newsprint and past the tick-tock clocks, and he put the Sun 660 casually down on the worktable a little too near the edge (just as Kevin had done in his own house after taking that first picture) and then just went on toward the stairs at the back which led up to his little apartment. There was a dusty old mirror propped against the wall back there, and Pop looked into it, watching to see if the boy or his father would pick the camera up or move it further away from the edge. He didn't think either would, but it was possible.

They spared it not so much as a passing glance and as Pop led them up the narrow stairway with the ancient eroded rubber treads he grinned in a way it would have been bad business for anyone to see and thought, *Damn, I'm good!*

He opened the door and they went into the apartment.

Neither John nor Kevin Delevan had ever been in Pop's private quarters, and John knew of no one who had. In a way this was not surprising; no one was ever going to nominate Pop as the town's number-one citizen. John thought it was not *impossible* that the old fuck had a friend or two—the world never exhausted its oddities, it seemed—but if so, he didn't know who they were.

And Kevin spared a fleeting thought for Mr. Baker, his favorite teacher. He wondered if, perchance, Mr. Baker had ever gotten into the sort of crack he'd need a fellow like Pop to get him out of. This seemed as unlikely to him as the idea of Pop having friends seemed to his father . . . but then, an hour ago the idea that his own father—

Well. It was best let go, perhaps.

Pop *did* have a friend (or at least an acquaintance) or two, but he didn't bring them here. He didn't want to. It was his place, and it came closer to revealing his true nature than he wanted anyone to see. It struggled to be neat and couldn't get there. The wallpaper was marked with water-stains; they weren't glaring, but stealthy and brown, like the phantom thoughts that trouble anxious minds. There were crusty dishes in the old-fashioned deep sink, and although the table was clean and the lid on the plastic waste-can was shut, there was an odor of sardines and something else—unwashed feet, maybe—which was almost not there. An odor as stealthy as the water-stains on the wallpaper.

The living room was tiny. Here the smell was not of sardines and (maybe) feet but of old pipe-smoke. Two windows looked out on nothing more scenic than the alley that ran behind Mulberry Street, and while their panes showed some signs of having been washed—at least swiped at occasionally—the corners were bleared and greasy with years of condensed smoke. The whole place had an air of nasty things swept under the faded hooked rugs and hidden beneath the old-fashioned, overstuffed easy-chair and sofa. Both of these articles were light green, and your eye wanted to tell you they matched but couldn't, because they didn't. Not quite.

The only new things in the room were a large Mitsubishi television with a twenty-five-inch screen and a VCR on the endtable beside it. To the left of the endtable was a rack which caught Kevin's eye because it was totally empty. Pop had thought it best to put the better than seventy fuck-movies he owned in the closet for the time being.

One video cassette rested on top of the television in an unmarked case.

"Sit down," Pop said, gesturing at the lumpy couch. He went over to the TV and slipped the cassette out of its case.

Mr. Delevan looked at the couch with a momentary expression of doubt, as if he thought it might have bugs, and then sat down gingerly. Kevin sat beside him. The fear was back, stronger than ever.

Pop turned on the VCR, slid the cassette in, and then pushed the carriage down. "I know a fellow up the city," he began (to residents of Castle Rock and its neighboring towns, "up the city" always meant Lewiston), "who's run a camera store for twenty years or so. He got into this VCR business as soon as it started up, said it was going to be the wave of the future. He wanted me to go halves with him, but I thought he was nuts. Well, I was wrong on that one, is what I mean to say, but—"

"Get to the point," Kevin's father said.

"I'm tryin," Pop said, wide-eyed and injured. "If you'll let me."

Kevin pushed his elbow gently against his father's side, and Mr. Delevan said no more.

"Anyway, a couple of years ago he found out rentin tapes for folks to watch wasn't the only way to make money with these gadgets. If you was willin to lay out as little as eight hundred bucks, you could take people's movies and snapshots and put em on a tape for em. Lots easier to watch."

Kevin made a little involuntary noise and Pop smiled and nodded.

"Ayuh. You took fifty-eight pitchers with that camera of yours, and we all saw each one was a little different than the last one, and I guess we knew what it meant, but I wanted to see for myself. You don't have to be from Missouri to say show me, is what I mean to say."

"You tried to make a movie out of those snapshots?" Mr. Delevan asked.

"Didn't *try*," Pop said. "*Did*. Or rather, the fella I know up the city did. But it was my idea."

"*Is* it a movie?" Kevin asked. He understood what Pop had done, and part of him was even chagrined that he hadn't thought of it himself, but mostly he was awash in wonder (and delight) at the idea.

"Look for yourself," Pop said, and turned on the TV. "Fifty-eight pitchers. When this fella does snapshots for folks, he generally videotapes each one for five seconds—long enough to get a good look, he says, but not long enough to get bored before you go on to the next one. I told him I wanted each of these on for just a single second, and to run them right together with no fades."

Kevin remembered a game he used to play in grade school when he had finished some lesson and had free time before the next one began. He had a little dime pad of paper which was called a Rain-Bo Skool Pad because there would be thirty pages of little yellow sheets, then thirty pages of little pink sheets, then thirty pages of green, and so on. To play the game, you went to the very last page and at the bottom you drew a stick-man wearing baggy shorts and holding his arms out. On the next page you drew the same stick-man in the same place and wearing the same baggy shorts, only this time you drew his arms further up . . . but just a little bit. You did that on every page until the arms came together over the stick-man's head. Then, if you still had time, you went on drawing the stick-man, but now with the arms going down. And if you flipped the pages very fast when you were done, you had a crude sort of cartoon which showed a boxer celebrating a KO: he raised his hands over his head, clasped them, shook them, lowered them.

He shivered. His father looked at him. Kevin shook his head and murmured, "Nothing."

"So what I mean to say is the tape only runs about a minute," Pop said. "You got to look close. Ready?"

No, Kevin thought.

"I guess so," Mr. Delevan said. He was still trying to sound grumpy and put-out, but Kevin could tell he had gotten interested in spite of himself.

"Okay," Pop Merrill said, and pushed the PLAY button.

Kevin told himself over and over again that it was stupid to feel scared. He told himself this and it didn't do a single bit of good.

He knew what he was going to see, because he and Meg had both noticed the Sun was doing something besides simply reproducing the same image over and over, like a photocopier; it did not take long for them to realize that the photographs were expressing movement from one to the next.

"Look," Meg had said. "The dog's moving!"

Instead of responding with one of the friendly-but-irritating wisecracks he usually reserved for his little sister, Kevin had said, "It *does* look like it . . . but you can't tell for sure, Meg."

"Yes, you can," she said. They were in his room, where he had been morosely looking at the camera. It sat on the middle of his desk with his new schoolbooks, which he had been meaning to cover, pushed to one side. Meg had bent the gooseneck of his study-lamp so it shone a bright circle of light on the middle of his desk blotter. She moved the camera aside and put the first picture—the one with the dab of cake-frosting on it—in the center of the light. "Count the fence-posts between the dog's behind and the righthand edge of the picture," she said.

"Those are pickets, not fence-posts," he told her. "Like what you do when your nose goes on strike."

"Ha-ha. Count them."

He did. He could see four, and part of a fifth, although the dog's scraggly hindquarters obscured most of that one.

"Now look at this one."

She put the fourth Polaroid in front of him. Now he could see *all* of the fifth picket, and part of the sixth.

So he knew—or believed—he was going to see a cross between a very old cartoon and one of those "flip-books" he used to make in grammar school when the time weighed heavy on his hands.

The last twenty-five seconds of the tape were indeed like that, although, Kevin thought, the flip-books he had drawn in the second grade were really better . . . the perceived action of the boxer raising and lowering his hands smoother. In the last twenty-five seconds of the videotape the action moved in rams and jerks which made the old Keystone Kops silent films look like marvels of modern filmmaking in comparison.

Still, the key word was *action,* and it held all of them—even Pop—spellbound. They watched the minute of footage three times without saying a word. There was no sound but breathing: Kevin's fast and smooth through his nose, his father's deeper, Pop's a phlegmy rattle in his narrow chest.

And the first thirty seconds or so . . .

He had expected action, he supposed; there was action in the flip-books, and there was action in the Saturday-morning cartoons, which were just a slightly more sophisticated version of the flip-books, but what he had not expected was that for the first thirty seconds of the tape it wasn't like watching notebook pages rapidly thumbed or even a primitive cartoon like *Possible Possum* on TV: for thirty seconds (twenty-eight, anyway), his single Polaroid photographs looked eerily like a real movie. Not a Hollywood movie, of course, not even a low-budget horror movie of the sort Megan sometimes pestered him to rent for their own VCR when their mother and father went out for the evening; it was more like a snippet of home movie made by someone who has just gotten an eight-millimeter camera and doesn't know how to use it very well yet.

In those first twenty-eight seconds, the black no-breed dog walked with barely perceptible jerks along the fence, exposing five, six, seven pickets; it even paused to sniff a second time at one of them, apparently reading another of those canine telegrams. Then it walked on, head down and toward the fence, hindquarters switched out toward the camera. And, halfway through this first part, Kevin noted something else he hadn't seen before: the photographer had apparently swung his camera to keep the dog in the frame. If he (or she) hadn't done so, the dog would have simply walked out of the picture, leaving nothing to look at but the fence. The pickets at the far right of the first two or three photographs disappeared beyond the righthand border of the picture and new pickets appeared at the left. You could tell, because the tip of one of those two rightmost pickets had been broken off. Now it was no longer in the frame.

The dog started to sniff again . . . and then its head came up. Its good ear stiffened; the one which had been slashed and laid limp in some long-ago fight tried to do the same. There was no sound, but Kevin felt with a certainty beyond repudiation that the dog had begun to growl. The dog had sensed something or someone. What or who?

Kevin looked at the shadow they had at first dismissed as the branch of a tree or maybe a phone-pole and knew.

Its head began to turn . . . and that was when the second half of this strange "film" began, thirty seconds of snap-jerk action that made your head ache and your eyeballs hot. Pop had had a hunch, Kevin thought, or maybe he had even read about something like this before. Either way, it had proved out and was too obvious to need stating. With the pictures taken quite closely together, if not exactly one after another, the action in the makeshift "movie" almost flowed. Not quite, but almost. But when the time between photographs was spaced, what they were watching became something that nauseated your eye because it wanted to see either a moving picture or a series of still photographs and instead it saw both and neither.

Time was passing in that flat Polaroid world. Not at the same speed it passed in this

(real?)

one, or the sun would have come up (or gone down) over there three times already and whatever the dog was going to do would be done (if it *had* something to do), and if it did not, it would just be gone and there would be only the moveless and seemingly eternal eroded picket fence guarding the listless patch of lawn, but it *was* passing.

The dog's head was coming around to face the photographer, owner of the shadow, like the head of a dog in the grip of a fit: at one moment the face and even the shape of the head was obscured by that floppy ear; then you saw one black-brown eye enclosed by a round and somehow mucky corona that made Kevin think of a spoiled egg-white; then you saw half the muzzle with the lips appearing slightly wrinkled, as if the dog were getting ready to bark or growl; and last of all you saw three-quarters of a face somehow more awful than the face of any mere dog had a right to be, even a mean one. The white spackles along its muzzle suggested it was no longer young. At the very end of the tape you saw the dog's lips were indeed pulling back. There was one blink of white Kevin thought was a tooth. He didn't see that until the third run-through. It was the eye that held him. It was homicidal. This breedless dog almost screamed rogue. And it was nameless; he knew that, as well. He knew beyond a shadow of a doubt that no Polaroid man or Polaroid woman or Polaroid child had ever named that Polaroid dog; it was a stray, born stray, raised stray, grown old and mean stray, the avatar of all the dogs who had ever wandered the world, unnamed and un-homed, killing chickens, eating garbage out of the cans they had long since learned to knock over, sleeping in culverts and beneath the porches of deserted houses. Its wits would be dim, but its instincts would be sharp and red. It—

When Pop Merrill spoke, Kevin was so deeply and fundamentally startled out of his thoughts that he nearly screamed.

"The man who took those pictures," he said. "If there *was* a person, is what I mean to say. What do you suppose happened to *him?*"

Pop had frozen the last frame with his remote control. A line of static ran through the picture. Kevin wished it ran through the dog's eye, but the line was below it. That eye stared out at them, baleful, stupidly murderous—no, not stupidly, not entirely, that was what made it not merely frightening but terrifying—and no one needed to answer Pop's question. You needed no more pictures to understand what was going to happen next. The dog had perhaps heard something: of course it had, and Kevin knew what. It had heard that squidgy little whine.

Further pictures would show it continuing to turn, and then beginning to fill more and more of each frame until there was nothing to see but dog—no listless patchy lawn, no fence, no sidewalk, no shadow. Just the dog.

Who meant to attack.

Who meant to kill, if it could.

Kevin's dry voice seemed to be coming from someone else. "I don't think it likes getting its picture taken," he said.

Pop's short laugh was like a bunch of dry twigs broken over a knee for kindling.

"Rewind it," Mr. Delevan said.

"You want to see the whole thing again?" Pop asked.

"No—just the last ten seconds or so."

Pop used the remote control to go back, then ran it again. The dog turned its head, as jerky as a robot which is old and running down but still dangerous, and Kevin wanted to tell them, *Stop now. Just stop. That's enough. Just stop and let's break the camera.* Because there was something else, wasn't there? Something he didn't want to think about but soon would, like it or not; he could feel it breaching in his mind like the broad back of a whale.

"Once more," Mr. Delevan said. "Frame by frame this time. Can you do that?"

"Ayuh," Pop said. "Goddam machine does everything but the laundry."

This time one frame, one picture, at a time. It was not like a robot now, or not exactly, but like some weird clock, something that belonged with Pop's other specimens downstairs. Jerk. Jerk. Jerk. The head coming around. Soon they would be faced by that merciless, not-quite-idiotic eye again.

"What's that?" Mr. Delevan asked.

"What's what?" Pop asked, as if he didn't know it was the thing the boy hadn't wanted to talk about the other day, the thing, he was convinced, that had made up the boy's mind about destroying the camera once and for all.

"Underneath its neck," Mr. Delevan said, and pointed. "It's not wearing a collar or a tag, but it's got something around its neck on a string or a thin rope."

"I dunno," Pop said imperturbably. "Maybe your boy does. Young folks have sharper eyes than us old fellas."

Mr. Delevan turned to look at Kevin. "Can you make it out?"

"I—" He fell silent. "It's really small."

His mind returned to what his father had said when they were leaving the house. *If she never asks you, you never have to tell*

her. . . . That's just the way we do things in the grown-up world.
Just now he had asked Kevin if he could make out what that
thing under the dog's neck was. Kevin hadn't really answered
that question; he had said something else altogether. *It's really
small.* And it was. The fact that he knew what it was in spite
of that . . . well . . .

What had his father called it? Skating up to the edge of a
lie?

And he *couldn't* actually see it. Not *actually.* Just the same,
he knew. The eye only suggested; the heart understood. Just
as his heart understood that, if he was right, the camera must
be destroyed. *Must* be.

At that moment, Pop Merrill was suddenly struck by an
agreeable inspiration. He got up and snapped off the TV.
"I've got the pitchers downstairs," he said. "Brought em back
with the videotape. I seen that thing m'self, and ran my magnifying glass over it, but still couldn't tell . . . but it *does*
look familiar, God cuss it. Just let me go get the pitchers and
m'glass."

"We might as well go down with you," Kevin said, which
was the last thing in the world Pop wanted, but then Delevan
stepped in, God bless him, and said he might like to look at
the tape again after they looked at the last couple of pictures
under the magnifying glass.

"Won't take a minute," Pop said, and was gone, sprightly as
a bird hopping from twig to twig on an apple tree, before either
of them could have protested, if either had had a mind to.

Kevin did not. That thought had finally breached its mon-
strous back in his mind, and, like it or not, he was forced to
contemplate it.

It was simple, as a whale's back is simple—at least to the
eye of one who does not study whales for a living—and it was
colossal in the same way.

It wasn't an idea but a simple certainty. It had to do with
that odd flatness Polaroids always seemed to have, with the

way they showed you things only in two dimensions, although all photographs did that; it was that other photographs seemed to at least *suggest* a third dimension, even those taken with a simple Kodak 110.

The things in *his* photographs, photographs which showed things he had never seen through the Sun's viewfinder or anywhere else, for that matter, were that same way: flatly, unapologetically two-dimensional.

Except for the dog.

The dog wasn't *flat.* The dog wasn't *meaningless,* a thing you could recognize but which had no emotional impact. The dog not only seemed to *suggest* three dimensions but to really *have* them, the way a hologram seems to really have them, or one of those 3-D movies where you had to wear special glasses to reconcile the double images.

It's not a Polaroid dog, Kevin thought, *and it doesn't belong in the world Polaroids take pictures of. That's crazy, I know it is, but I also know it's true. So what does it mean? Why is my camera taking pictures of it over and over . . . and what Polaroid man or Polaroid woman is snapping pictures of it? Does he or she even see it? If it is a three-dimensional dog in a two-dimensional world, maybe he or she doesn't see it . . . can't see it. They say for us time is the fourth dimension, and we know it's there, but we can't see it. We can't even really feel it pass, although sometimes, especially when we're bored, I guess, it seems like we can.*

But when you got right down to it, all that might not even matter, and the questions were far too tough for him, anyway. There were other questions that seemed more important to him, vital questions, maybe even mortal ones.

Like why was the dog in *his* camera?

Did it want something of *him,* or just of anybody? At first he had thought the answer was anybody, anybody would do because anybody could take pictures of it and the movement always advanced. But the thing around its neck, that thing that wasn't a collar . . . that had to do with him, Kevin Delevan, and nobody else. Did it want to do something *to* him? If the answer to *that* question was yes, you could forget all the other ones, because it was pretty goddamned obvious what the dog wanted to do. It was in its murky eye, in the snarl you could just see beginning. He thought it wanted two things.

First to escape.

Then to kill.

There's a man or woman over there with a camera who maybe doesn't even see that dog, Kevin thought, *and if the photographer can't see the dog, maybe the dog can't see the photographer, and so the photographer is safe. But if the dog really is three-dimensional, maybe he sees out—maybe he sees whoever is using my camera. Maybe it's still not me, or not specifically me; maybe whoever is using the camera is its target.*

Still—the thing it was wearing around its neck. What about that?

He thought of the cur's dark eyes, saved from stupidity by a single malevolent spark. God knew how the dog had gotten into that Polaroid world in the first place, but when its picture was taken, it could see *out,* and it wanted to *get* out, and Kevin believed in his heart that it wanted to kill him first, the thing it was wearing around its neck *said* it wanted to kill him first, *proclaimed* that it wanted to kill him first, but after that?

Why, after Kevin, anyone would do.

Anyone at all.

In a way it was like another game you played when you were a little kid, wasn't it? It was like Giant Step. The dog had been walking along the fence. The dog had heard the Polaroid, that squidgy little whine. It turned, and saw . . . what? Its own world or universe? A world or universe enough *like* its own so it saw or sensed it could or at least might be able to live and hunt here? It didn't matter. Now, every time someone took a picture of it, the dog would get closer. It would get closer and closer until . . . well, until what? Until it burst through, somehow?

"That's stupid," he muttered. "It'd never fit."

"What?" his father asked, roused from his own musings.

"Nothing," Kevin said. "I was just talking to myse—"

Then, from downstairs, muffled but audible, they heard Pop Merrill cry out in mingled dismay, irritation, and surprise: "Well shit fire and save matches! *Goddammit!*"

Kevin and his father looked at each other, startled.

"Let's go see what happened," his father said, and got up. "I hope he didn't fall down and break his arm, or something. I mean, part of me *does* hope it, but . . . you know."

Kevin thought: *What if he's been taking pictures? What if that dog's down there?*

It hadn't sounded like fear in the old man's voice, and of course there really was no way a dog that looked as big as a medium-sized German shepherd could come through either a camera the size of the Sun 660 or one of the prints it made. You might as well try to drag a washing machine through a knothole.

Still, he felt fear enough for both of them—for all three of them—as he followed his father back down the stairs to the gloomy bazaar below.

Going down the stairs, Pop Merrill was as happy as a clam at high tide.

He had been prepared to make the switch right in front of them if he had to. Might have been a problem if it had just been the boy, who was still a year or so away from thinking he knew everything, but the boy's dad—ah, fooling *that* fine fellow would have been like stealing a bottle from a baby. Had he told the boy about the jam he'd gotten into that time? From the way the boy looked at him—a new, cautious way—Pop thought Delevan probably had. And what else had the father told the son? Well, let's see. *Does he let you call him Pop? That means he's planning to pull a fast one on you.* That was for starters. *He's a lowdown snake in the grass, son.* That was for seconds.

73

And, of course, there was the prize of them all: *Let me do the talking, boy. I know him better than you do. You just let me handle everything.* Men like Delevan were to Pop Merrill what a nice platter of fried chicken was to some folks—tender, tasty, juicy, and all but falling off the bone. Once Delevan had been little more than a kid himself, and he would never fully understand that it wasn't Pop who had stuck his tit in the wringer but he himself. The man could have gone to his wife and she would have tapped that old biddy aunt of hers whose tight little ass was lined with hundred-dollar bills, and Delevan would have spent some time in the doghouse, but she would have let him out in time. He not only hadn't seen it that way; he hadn't seen it at all. And now, for no reason but idiot time, which came and went without any help from anyone, he thought he knew all there was to know about Reginald Marion Merrill.

Which was just the way Pop liked it.

Why, he could have swapped one camera for the other right in front of the man and Delevan never would have seen a god-damned thing—that was how sure he was he had old Pop figured out.

But this was better.

You never ever asked Lady Luck for a date; she had a way of standing men up just when they needed her the most. But if she showed up on her own . . . well, it was wise to drop whatever it was you were doing and take her out and wine her and dine her just as lavishly as you could. That was one bitch who always put out if you treated her right.

So he went quickly to the worktable, bent, and extracted the Polaroid 660 with the broken lens from the shadows underneath. He put it on the table, fished a key-ring from his pocket (with one quick glance over his shoulder to be sure neither of them had decided to come down after all), and selected the small key which opened the locked drawer that formed the entire left side of the table. In this deep drawer were a number of gold Krugerrands; a stamp album in which the least valuable stamp was worth six hundred dollars in the latest *Scott Stamp Catalogue*; a coin collection worth approximately nineteen thousand dollars; two dozen glossy photographs of a bleary-eyed woman having sexual congress with a Shetland pony; and an amount of cash totalling just over two thousand dollars.

The cash, which he stowed in a variety of tin cans, was Pop's loan-out money. John Delevan would have recognized the bills. They were all crumpled tens.

Pop deposited Kevin's Sun 660 in this drawer, locked it, and put his key-ring back in his pocket. Then he pushed the camera with the broken lens off the edge of the worktable (again) and cried out "Well shit fire and save matches! *Goddammit!*" loud enough for them to hear.

Then he arranged his face in the proper expression of dismay and chagrin and waited for them to come running to see what had happened.

"Pop?" Kevin cried. "Mr. Merrill? Are you okay?"

"Ayuh," he said. "Didn't hurt nothin but my goddam pride. That camera's just bad luck, I guess. I bent over to open the tool-drawer, is what I mean to say, and I knocked the fucking thing right off onto the floor. Only I guess it didn't come through s'well this time. I dunno if I should say I'm sorry or not. I mean, you was gonna—"

He held the camera apologetically out to Kevin, who took it, looked at the broken lens and shattered plastic of the housing around it. "No, it's okay," Kevin told him, turning the camera over in his hands—but he did not handle it in the same gingerly, tentative way he had before: as if it might really be constructed not of plastic and glass but some sort of explosive. "I meant to bust it up, anyhow."

"Guess I saved you the trouble."

"I'd feel better—" Kevin began.

"Ayuh, ayuh. I feel the same way about mice. Laugh if you want to, but when I catch one in a trap and it's dead, I beat it with a broom anyway. Just to be sure, is what I mean to say."

Kevin smiled faintly, then looked at his father. "He said he's got a chopping block out back, Dad—"

"Got a pretty good sledge in the shed, too, if ain't nobody took it."

"Do you mind, Dad?"

"It's your camera, Kev," Delevan said. He flicked a distrustful glance at Pop, but it was a glance that said he distrusted Pop on general principles, and not for any specific reason. "But if it will make you feel any better, I think it's the right decision."

"Good," Kevin said. He felt a tremendous weight go off his shoulders—no, it was from his *heart* that the weight was lifted. With the lens broken, the camera was surely useless . . . but he wouldn't feel really at ease until he saw it in fragments around Pop's chopping block. He turned it over in his hands, front to back and back to front, amused and amazed at how much he liked the broken way it looked and felt.

"I think I owe you the cost of that camera, Delevan," Pop said, knowing exactly how the man would respond.

"No," Delevan said. "Let's smash it and forget this whole crazy thing ever hap—" He paused. "I almost forgot—we were going to look at those last few photos under your magnifying glass. I wanted to see if I could make out the thing the dog's wearing. I keep thinking it looks familiar."

"We can do that after we get rid of the camera, can't we?" Kevin asked. "Okay, Dad?"

"Sure."

"And then," Pop said, "it might not be such a bad idear to burn the pitchers themselves. You could do it right in my stove."

"I think that's a *great* idea," Kevin said. "What do you think, Dad?"

"I think Mrs. Merrill never raised any fools," his father said.

"Well," Pop said, smiling enigmatically from behind folds of rising blue smoke, "there was five of us, you know."

• • •

The day had been bright blue when Kevin and his father walked down to the Emporium Galorium; a perfect autumn day. Now it was four-thirty, the sky had mostly clouded over, and it looked like it might rain before dark. The first real chill of the fall touched Kevin's hands. It would chap them red if he stayed out long enough, but he had no plans to. His mom would be home in half an hour, and already he wondered what she would say when she saw Dad was with him, and what his dad would say.

But that was for later.

Kevin set the Sun 660 on the chopping block in the little backyard, and Pop Merrill handed him a sledgehammer. The haft was worn smooth with usage. The head was rusty, as if someone had left it carelessly out in the rain not once or twice but many times. Yet it would do the job, all right. Kevin had no doubt of that. The Polaroid, its lens broken and most of the housing around it shattered as well, looked fragile and defenseless sitting there on the block's chipped, chunked, and splintered surface, where you expected to see a length of ash or maple waiting to be split in two.

Kevin set his hands on the sledgehammer's smooth handle and tightened them.

"You're sure, son?" Mr. Delevan asked.

"Yes."

"Okay." Kevin's father glanced at his own watch. "Do it, then."

Pop stood to one side with his pipe clamped between his wretched teeth, hands in his back pockets. He looked shrewdly from the boy to the man and then back to the boy, but said nothing.

Kevin lifted the sledgehammer and, suddenly surprised by an anger at the camera he hadn't even known he felt, he brought it down with all the force he could muster.

Too hard, he thought. *You're going to miss it, be lucky not to*

77

mash your own foot, and there it will sit, not much more than a piece of hollow plastic a little kid could stomp flat without half trying, and even if you're lucky enough to miss your foot, Pop will look at you. He won't say anything: he won't have to. It'll all be in the way he looks at you.

And thought also: *It doesn't matter if I hit it or not. It's magic, some kind of magic camera, and you* CAN'T *break it. Even if you hit it dead on the money the sledge will just bounce off it, like bullets off Superman's chest.*

But then there was no more time to think anything, because the sledge connected squarely with the camera. Kevin really *had* swung much too hard to maintain anything resembling control, but he got lucky. And the sledgehammer didn't just bounce back up, maybe hitting Kevin square between the eyes and killing him, like the final twist in a horror story.

The Sun didn't so much shatter as detonate. Black plastic flew everywhere. A long rectangle with a shiny black square at one end—a picture which would never be taken, Kevin supposed—fluttered to the bare ground beside the chopping block and lay there, face-down.

There was a moment of silence so complete they could hear not only the cars on Lower Main Street but kids playing tag half a block away in the parking lot behind Wardell's Country Store, which had gone bankrupt two years before and had stood vacant ever since.

"Well, that's *that*," Pop said. "You swung that sledge just like Paul Bunyan, Kevin! I should smile n kiss a pig if you didn't.

"No need to do that," he said, now addressing Mr. Delevan, who was picking up broken chunks of plastic as prissily as a man picking up the pieces of a glass he has accidentally knocked to the floor and shattered. "I have a boy comes in and cleans up the yard every week or two. I know it don't look like much as it is, but if I didn't have that kid . . . Glory!"

"Then maybe we ought to use your magnifying glass and take

78

a look at those pictures," Mr. Delevan said, standing up. He dropped the few pieces of plastic he had picked up into a rusty incinerator that stood nearby and then brushed off his hands.

"Fine by me," Pop said.

"Then burn them," Kevin reminded. "Don't forget that."

"I didn't," Pop said. "I'll feel better when they're gone, too."

"Jesus!" John Delevan said. He was bending over Pop Merrill's worktable, looking through the lighted magnifying glass at the second-to-last photograph. It was the one in which the object around the dog's neck showed most clearly; in the last photo, the object had swung back in the other direction again. "Kevin, look at that and tell me if it's what I think it is."

Kevin took the magnifying glass and looked. He had known, of course, but even so it still wasn't a look just for form's sake. Clyde Tombaugh must have looked at an actual photograph of the planet Pluto for the first time with the same fascination. Tombaugh had known it was there; calculations showing similar distortions in the orbital paths of Neptune and Uranus had made Pluto not just a possibility but a necessity. Still, to *know* a thing was there, even to know what it *was* . . . that did not detract from the fascination of actually *seeing* it for the first time.

He let go of the switch and handed the glass back to Pop. "Yeah," he said to his father. "It's what you think it is." His voice was as flat as . . . as flat as the things in that Polaroid world, he supposed, and he felt an urge to laugh. He kept the sound inside, not because it would have been inappropriate to laugh (although he supposed it would have been) but because the sound would have come out sounding . . . well . . . flat.

Pop waited and when it became clear to him they were going to need a nudge, he said: "Well, don't keep me hoppin from one foot to the other! What the hell is it?"

Kevin had felt reluctant to tell him before, and he felt reluctant now. There was no reason for it, but—

Stop being so goddamned dumb! He helped you when you needed helping, no matter how he earns his dough. Tell him and burn the pictures and let's get out of here before all those clocks start striking five.

Yes. If he was around when *that* happened, he thought it would be the final touch; he would just go completely bananas and they could cart him away to Juniper Hill, raving about real dogs in Polaroid worlds and cameras that took the same picture over and over again except not quite.

"The Polaroid camera was a birthday present," he heard himself saying in that same dry voice. "What it's wearing around its neck was another one."

Pop slowly pushed his glasses up onto his bald head and squinted at Kevin. "I don't guess I'm followin you, son."

"I have an aunt," Kevin said. "Actually she's my great-aunt, but we're not supposed to call her that, because she says it makes her feel old. Aunt Hilda. Anyway, Aunt Hilda's husband left her a lot of money—my mom says she's worth over a million dollars—but she's a tightwad."

He stopped, leaving his father space to protest, but his father only smiled sourly and nodded. Pop Merrill, who knew all about *that* situation (there was not, in truth, much in Castle Rock and the surrounding areas Pop didn't know at least something about), simply held his peace and waited for the boy to get around to spilling it.

"She comes and spends Christmas with us once every three years, and that's about the only time we go to church, because *she* goes to church. We have lots of broccoli when Aunt Hilda comes. None of us like it, and it just about makes my sister puke, but Aunt Hilda likes broccoli a *lot,* so we have it. There was a book on our summer reading list, *Great Expectations,* and there was a lady in it who was just like Aunt Hilda. She got her kicks dangling her money in front of her relatives. Her name was Miss Havisham, and when Miss Havisham said frog, people jumped. We jump, and I guess the rest of our family does, too."

"Oh, your Uncle Randy makes your mother look like a piker," Mr. Delevan said unexpectedly. Kevin thought his dad meant it to sound amused in a cynical sort of way, but what came through was a deep, acidic bitterness. "When Aunt Hilda says frog in Randy's house, they all just about turn cartwheels over the roofbeams."

"Anyway," Kevin told Pop, "she sends me the same thing for my birthday every year. I mean, each one is different, but each one's really the same."

"What is it she sends you, boy?"

"A string tie," Kevin said. "Like the kind you see guys wearing in old-time country-music bands. It has something different on the clasp every year, but it's always a string tie."

Pop snatched the magnifying glass and bent over the picture with it. "Stone the crows!" he said, straightening up. "A string tie! That's just what it is! Now how come I didn't see that?"

"Because it isn't the sort of thing a dog would wear around his neck, I guess," Kevin said in that same wooden voice. They had been here for only forty-five minutes or so, but he felt as if he had aged another fifteen years. *The thing to remember,* his mind told him over and over, *is that the camera is gone. It's nothing but splinters. Never mind all the King's horses and all the King's men; not even all the guys who work making cameras at the Polaroid factory in Schenectady could put* that *baby back together again.*

Yes, and thank God. Because this was the end of the line. As far as Kevin was concerned, if he never encountered *the supernatural* again until he was eighty, never so much as brushed up against it, it would still be too soon.

"Also, it's very small," Mr. Delevan pointed out. "I was there when Kevin took it out of the box, and we all knew what it was going to be. The only mystery was what would be on the clasp this year. We joked about it."

"What *is* on the clasp?" Pop asked, peering into the photograph again . . . or peering *at* it, anyway: Kevin would testify in any court in the land that peering *into* a Polaroid was simply impossible.

"A bird," Kevin said. "I'm pretty sure it's a woodpecker. And that's what the dog in the picture is wearing around its neck. A string tie with a woodpecker on the clasp."

"Jesus!" Pop said. He was in his own quiet way one of the world's finer actors, but there was no need to simulate the surprise he felt now.

Mr. Delevan abruptly swept all the Polaroids together. "Let's put these goddam things in the woodstove," he said.

When Kevin and his father got home, it was ten minutes past five and starting to drizzle. Mrs. Delevan's two-year-old Toyota was not in the driveway, but she had been and gone. There was a note from her on the kitchen table, held down by the salt and pepper shakers. When Kevin unfolded the note, a ten-dollar bill fell out.

Dear Kevin,

    At the bridge game Jane Doyon asked if Meg and I would like to have dinner with her at Bonanza as her husband is off to Pittsburgh on business and she's knocking around the house alone. I said we'd be delighted. Meg especially. You know how much she likes to be "one of the girls"! Hope you don't mind eating in "solitary splendor." Why not order a pizza & some soda for yourself, and your father can order for himself when he gets home. He doesn't like reheated pizza & you know he'll want a couple of beers.

Luv you,
Mom

They looked at each other, both saying *Well, there's one thing we don't have to worry about* without having to say it out loud.

Apparently neither she nor Meg had noticed that Mr. Delevan's car was still in the garage.

"Do you want me to—" Kevin began, but there was no need to finish because his father cut across him: "Yes. Check. Right now."

Kevin went up the stairs by twos and into his room. He had a bureau and a desk. The bottom desk drawer was full of what Kevin simply thought of as "stuff": things it would have seemed somehow criminal to throw away, although he had no real use for any of them. There was his grandfather's pocket-watch, heavy, scrolled, magnificent . . . and so badly rusted that the jeweler in Lewiston he and his mother had brought it to only took one look, shook his head, and pushed it back across the counter. There were two sets of matching cufflinks and two orphans, a *Penthouse* gatefold, a paperback book called *Gross Jokes,* and a Sony Walkman which had for some reason developed a habit of eating the tapes it was supposed to play. It was just stuff, that was all. There was no other word that fit.

Part of the stuff, of course, was the thirteen string ties Aunt Hilda had sent him for his last thirteen birthdays.

He took them out one by one, counted, came up with twelve instead of thirteen, rooted through the stuff-drawer again, then counted again. Still twelve.

"Not there?"

Kevin, who had been squatting, cried out and leaped to his feet.

"I'm sorry," Mr. Delevan said from the doorway. "That was dumb."

"That's okay," Kevin said. He wondered briefly how fast a person's heart could beat before the person in question simply blew his engine. "I'm just . . . on edge. Stupid."

"It's not." His father looked at him soberly. "When I saw that tape, I got so scared I felt like maybe I'd have to reach into my mouth and push my stomach back down with my fingers."

83

Kevin looked at his father gratefully.

"It's not there, is it?" Mr. Delevan asked. "The one with the woodpecker or whatever in hell it was supposed to be?"

"No. It's not."

"Did you keep the camera in that drawer?"

Kevin nodded his head slowly. "Pop—Mr. Merrill—said to let it rest every so often. That was part of the schedule he made out."

Something tugged briefly at his mind, was gone.

"So I stuck it in there."

"Boy," Mr. Delevan said softly.

"Yeah."

They looked at each other in the gloom, and then suddenly Kevin smiled. It was like watching the sun burst through a raft of clouds.

"What?"

"I was remembering how it felt," Kevin said. "I swung that sledgehammer so hard—"

Mr. Delevan began to smile, too. "I thought you were going to take off your own damned—"

"—and when it hit it made this CRUNCH! sound—"

"—flew every damn whichway—"

"BOOM!" Kevin finished. "Gone!"

They began to laugh together in Kevin's room, and Kevin found he was almost—*almost*—glad all this had happened. The sense of relief was as inexpressible and yet as perfect as the sensation one feels when, either by happy accident or by some psychic guidance, another person manages to scratch that one itchy place on one's back that one cannot scratch oneself, hitting it exactly, bang on the money, making it wonderfully worse for a single second by the simple touch, pressure, arrival, of those fingers . . . and then, oh blessed relief.

It was like that with the camera and with his father's knowing.

"It's gone," Kevin said. "Isn't it?"

"As gone as Hiroshima after the *Enola Gay* dropped the

A-bomb on it," Mr. Delevan replied, and then added: "Smashed to shit, is what I mean to say."

Kevin gawped at his father and then burst into helpless peals—screams, almost—of laughter. His father joined him. They orderd a loaded pizza shortly after. When Mary and Meg Delevan arrived home at twenty past seven, they both still had the giggles.

"Well, you two look like you've been up to no good," Mrs. Delevan said, a little puzzled. There was something in their hilarity that struck the woman center of her—that deep part which the sex seems to tap into fully only in times of child-birth and disaster—as a little unhealthy. They looked and sounded like men who may have just missed having a car acci-dent. "Want to let the ladies in on it?"

"Just two bachelors having a good time," Mr. Delevan said.

"*Smashing* good time," Kevin amplified, to which his father added, "Is what we mean to say," and they looked at each other and were howling again.

Meg, honestly bewildered, looked at her mother and said: "Why are they doing that, Mom?"

Mrs. Delevan said, "Because they have penises, dear. Go hang up your coat."

Pop Merrill let the Delevans, *père et fils,* out, and then locked the door behind them. He turned off all the lights save for the one over the worktable, produced his keys, and opened his own stuff-drawer. From it he took Kevin Delevan's Polaroid Sun 660, chipped but otherwise undamaged, and looked at it fixedly. It had scared both the father and the son. That was clear enough to Pop; it had scared him as well, and still did. But to put a thing like this on a block and smash it to smith-ereens? That was crazy.

There was a way to turn a buck on this goddam thing.

There always was.

Pop locked it away in the drawer. He would sleep on it, and

by the morning he would know how to proceed. In truth, he already had a pretty goddam good idea.

He got up, snapped off the work-light, and wove his way through the gloom toward the steps leading up to his apartment. He moved with the unthinking surefooted grace of long practice.

Halfway there, he stopped.

He felt an urge, an amazingly strong urge, to go back and look at the camera again. What in God's name for? He didn't even have any *film* for the Christless thing . . . not that *he* had any intentions of taking any pictures with it. If someone *else* wanted to take some snapshots, watch that dog's progress, the buyer was welcome. Caveet emperor, as he always said. Let the goddam emperor caveet or not as it suited him. As for him, he'd as soon go into a cage filled with lions without even a goddam whip and chair.

Still . . .

"Leave it," he said roughly in the darkness, and the sound of his own voice startled him and got him moving and he went upstairs without another look back.

CHAPTER SEVEN

Very early the next morning, Kevin Delevan had a nightmare so horrible he could only remember parts of it, like isolated phrases of music heard on a radio with a defective speaker.

He was walking into a grungy little mill-town. Apparently he was on the bum, because he had a pack on his back. The name of the town was Oatley, and Kevin had the idea it was either in Vermont or upstate New York. *You know anyone hiring here in Oatley?* he asked an old man pushing a shopping-cart along a cracked sidewalk. There were no groceries in the cart; it was full of indeterminate junk, and Kevin realized the man was a wino. *Get away!* the wino screamed. *Get away! Feef! Fushing feef! Fushing FEEF!*

Kevin ran, darted across the street, more frightened of the man's madness than he was of the idea anyone might believe that he, Kevin, was a thief. The wino called after him: *This ain't Oatley! This is Hildasville! Get out of town, you fushing feef!*

It was then that he realized that this town wasn't Oatley or Hildasville or any other town with a normal name. How could an utterly abnormal town have a normal name?

Everything—streets, buildings, cars, signs, the few pedestrians—was two-dimensional. Things had height, they had width . . . but they had no thickness. He passed a woman who looked the way Meg's ballet teacher might look if the ballet teacher put on a hundred and fifty pounds. She was wearing slacks the color of Bazooka bubble gum. Like the wino, she was pushing a shopping-cart. It had a squeaky wheel. It was full of Polaroid Sun 660 cameras. She looked at Kevin with narrow suspicion as they drew closer together. At the moment when they passed each other on the sidewalk, she disappeared. Her *shadow* was still there and he could still hear that rhythmic squeaking, but she was no longer there. Then she reappeared, looking back at him from her fat flat suspicious face, and Kevin understood the reason why she had disappeared for a moment. It was because the concept of "a side view" didn't exist, *couldn't* exist, in a world where everything was perfectly flat.

This is Polaroidsville, he thought with a relief which was strangely mingled with horror. *And that means this is only a dream.*

Then he saw the white picket fence, and the dog, and the photographer standing in the gutter. There were rimless spectacles propped up on his head. It was Pop Merrill.

Well, son, you found him, the two-dimensional Polaroid Pop said to Kevin without removing his eye from the shutter. *That's the dog, right there. The one tore up that kid out in Schenectady.* YOUR *dog, is what I mean to say.*

Then Kevin woke up in his own bed, afraid he had screamed but more concerned at first not about the dream but to make sure he was *all there,* all three dimensions of him.

He was. But something was wrong.

Stupid dream, he thought. *Let it go, why can't you? It's over. Photos are burned, all fifty-eight of them. And the camera's bus—*

His thought broke off like ice as that something, that something *wrong,* teased at his mind again.

It's not over, he thought. *It's n—*

But before the thought could finish itself, Kevin Delevan fell deeply, dreamlessly asleep. The next morning, he barely remembered the nightmare at all.

CHAPTER EIGHT

The two weeks following his acquisition of Kevin Delevan's Polaroid Sun were the most aggravating, infuriating, *humiliating* two weeks of Pop Merrill's life. There were quite a few people in Castle Rock who would have said it couldn't have happened to a more deserving guy. Not that anyone in Castle Rock did know . . . and that was just about all the consolation Pop could take. He found it cold comfort. Very cold indeed, thank you very much.

But who would have ever believed the Mad Hatters would have, *could* have, let him down so badly?

It was almost enough to make a man wonder if he was starting to slip a little.

God forbid.

CHAPTER NINE

Back in September, he hadn't even bothered to wonder if he would sell the Polaroid; the only questions were how soon and how much. The Delevans had bandied the word *supernatural* about, and Pop hadn't corrected them, although he knew that what the Sun was doing would be more properly classed by psychic investigators as a paranormal rather than supernatural phenomenon. He *could* have told them that, but if he *had*, they might both have wondered how come the owner of a small-town used-goods store (and part-time usurer) knew so much about the subject. The fact was this: he knew a lot because it was *profitable* to know a lot, and it was profitable to know a lot because of the people he thought of as "my Mad Hatters."

Mad Hatters were people who recorded empty rooms on expensive audio equipment not for a lark or a drunken party stunt, but either because they believed passionately in an unseen world and wanted to prove its existence, or because they wanted passionately to get in touch with friends and/or relatives who had "passed on" ("passed on": that's what they always called it; Mad Hatters never had relatives who did something so simple as die).

Mad Hatters not only owned and used Ouija Boards, they had regular conversations with "spirit guides" in the "other world" (never "heaven," "hell," or even "the rest area of the dead" but the "other world") who put them in touch with friends, relatives, queens, dead rock-and-roll singers, even arch-villains. Pop knew of a Mad Hatter in Vermont who had twice-weekly conversations with Hitler. Hitler had told him it was all a bum rap, he had sued for peace in January of 1943

90

and that son of a bitch Churchill had turned him down. Hitler had also told him Paul Newman was a space alien who had been born in a cave on the moon.

Mad Hatters went to séances as regularly (and as compulsively) as drug addicts visited their pushers. They bought crystal balls and amulets guaranteed to bring good luck; they organized their own little societies and investigated reputedly haunted houses for all the usual phenomena: teleplasm, table-rappings, floating tables and beds, cold spots, and, of course, ghosts. They noted all of these, real or imagined, with the enthusiasm of dedicated bird-watchers.

Most of them had a ripping good time. Some did not. There was that fellow from Wolfeboro, for instance. He hanged himself in the notorious Tecumseh House, where a gentleman farmer had, in the 1880s and '90s, helped his fellow men by day and helped himself to them by night, dining on them at a formal table in his cellar. The table stood upon a floor of sour packed dirt which had yielded the bones and decomposed bodies of at least twelve and perhaps as many as thirty-five young men, all vagabonds. The fellow from Wolfeboro had left this brief note on a pad of paper beside his Ouija Board: *Can't leave the house. Doors all locked. I hear him eating. Tried cotton. Does no good.*

And the poor deluded asshole probably thought he really did, Pop had mused after hearing this story from a source he trusted.

Then there was a fellow in Dunwich, Massachusetts, to whom Pop had once sold a so-called spirit trumpet for ninety dollars; the fellow had taken the trumpet to the Dunwich Cemetery and must have heard something exceedingly unpleasant, because he had been raving in a padded cell in Arkham for almost six years now, totally insane. When he had gone into the boneyard, his hair had been black; when his screams awoke the few neighbors who lived close enough to the cemetery to hear them and the police were summoned, it was as white as his howling face.

And there was the woman in Portland who lost an eye when

a session with the Ouija Board went cataclysmically wrong . . . the man in Kingston, Rhode Island, who lost three fingers on his right hand when the rear door of a car in which two teenagers had committed suicide closed on it . . . the old lady who landed in Massachusetts Memorial Hospital short most of one ear when her equally elderly cat, Claudette, supposedly went on a rampage during a séance . . .

Pop believed some of these things, disbelieved others, and mostly held no opinion—not because he didn't have enough hard evidence one way or the other, but because he didn't give a fart in a high wind about ghosts, séances, crystal balls, spirit trumpets, rampaging cats, or the fabled John the Con-querer Root. As far as Reginald Marion "Pop" Merrill was concerned, the Mad Hatters could all take a flying fuck at the moon.

As long, of course, as one of them handed over some mighty tall tickets for Kevin Delevan's camera before taking passage on the next shuttle.

Pop didn't call these enthusiasts Mad Hatters because of their spectral interests; he called them that because the great majority—he was sometimes tempted to say *all* of them—seemed to be rich, retired, and just begging to be plucked. If you were willing to spend fifteen minutes with them nodding and agreeing while they assured you they could pick a fake medium from a real one just by walking into the *room,* let alone sitting down at the séance table, or if you spent an equal amount of time listening to garbled noises which might or might not be words on a tape player with the proper expression of awe on your face, you could sell them a four-dollar paperweight for a hundred by telling them a man had once glimpsed his dead mother in it. You gave them a smile and they wrote you a check for two hundred dollars. You gave them an encouraging word and they wrote you a check for two *thousand* dollars. If you gave them both things at the same time, they just kind of passed the checkbook over to you and asked you to fill in an amount.

It had always been as easy as taking candy from a baby.
Until now.

Pop didn't keep a file in his cabinet marked MAD HATTERS any
more than he kept one marked COIN COLLECTORS or STAMP
COLLECTORS. He didn't even *have* a file-cabinet. The closest
thing to it was a battered old book of phone numbers he carried around in his back pocket (which, like his purse, had over
the years taken on the shallow ungenerous curve of the spin-
dly buttock it lay against every day). Pop kept his files where a
man in his line of work should *always* keep them: in his head.
There were eight full-blown Mad Hatters that he had done
business with over the years, people who didn't just dabble in
the occult but who got right down and rolled around in it. The
richest was a retired industrialist named McCarty who lived
on his own island about twelve miles off the coast. This fellow
disdained boats and employed a full-time pilot who flew him
back and forth to the mainland when he needed to go.

Pop went to see him on September 28th, the day after he
obtained the camera from Kevin (he didn't, couldn't, exactly
think of it as robbery; the boy, after all, had been planning
to smash it to shit anyway, and what he didn't know surely
couldn't hurt him). He drove to a private airstrip just north of
Boothbay Harbor in his old but perfectly maintained car, then
gritted his teeth and slitted his eyes and held onto the steel
lockbox with the Polaroid Sun 660 in it for dear life as the
Mad Hatter's Beechcraft plunged down the dirt runway like
a rogue horse, rose into the air just as Pop was sure they were
going to fall off the edge and be smashed to jelly on the rocks
below, and flew away into the autumn empyrean. He had made
this trip twice before, and had sworn each time that he would
never get into that goddam flying coffin again.

They bumped and jounced along with the hungry Atlantic
less than five hundred feet below, the pilot talking cheerfully
the whole way. Pop nodded and said ayuh in what seemed like

the right places, although he was more concerned with his imminent demise than with anything the pilot was saying.

Then the island was ahead with its horribly, dismally, suicidally short landing strip and its sprawling house of redwood and fieldstone, and the pilot swooped down, leaving Pop's poor old acid-shrivelled stomach somewhere in the air above them, and they hit with a thud and then, somehow, miraculously, they were taxiing to a stop, still alive and whole, and Pop could safely go back to believing God was just another invention of the Mad Hatters . . . at least until he had to get back in that damned plane for the return journey.

"Great day for flying, huh, Mr. Merrill?" the pilot asked, unfolding the steps for him.

"Finest kind," Pop grunted, then strode up the walk to the house where the Thanksgiving turkey stood in the doorway, smiling in eager anticipation. Pop had promised to show him "the goddamnedest thing I ever come across," and Cedric McCarty looked like he couldn't wait. He'd take one quick look for form's sake, Pop thought, and then fork over the lettuce. He went back to the mainland forty-five minutes later, barely noticing the thumps and jounces and gut-goozling drops as the Beech hit the occasional air-pocket. He was a chastened, thoughtful man.

He had aimed the Polaroid at the Mad Hatter and took his picture. While they waited for it to develop, the Mad Hatter took a picture of Pop . . . and when the flashbulb went off, had he heard something? Had he heard the low, ugly snarl of that black dog, or had it been his imagination? Imagination, most likely. Pop had made some magnificent deals in his time, and you couldn't do that without imagination.

Still—

Cedric McCarty, retired industrialist *par excellence* and Mad Hatter *extraordinaire,* watched the photographs develop with that same childlike eagerness, but when they finally came clear, he looked amused and even perhaps a little contemptuous and Pop knew with the infallible intuition which had developed over almost fifty years that arguing, cajolery, even vague hints that he had another customer just *slavering* for a chance to buy this camera—none of those usually reliable techniques would work. A big orange NO SALE card had gone up in Cedric McCarty's mind.

By why?

Goddammit, *why?*

In the picture Pop took, that glint Kevin had spotted amid the wrinkles of the black dog's muzzle had clearly become a tooth—except *tooth* wasn't the right word, not by any stretch of the imagination. That was a *fang*. In the one McCarty took, you could see the beginnings of the neighboring teeth.

Fucking dog's got a mouth like a bear-trap, Pop thought. Unbidden, an image of his arm in that dog's mouth rose in his mind. He saw the dog not *biting* it, not *eating* it, but *shredding* it, the way the many teeth of a wood-chipper shred bark, leaves, and small branches. *How long would it take?* he wondered, and looked at those dirty eyes staring out at him from the overgrown face and knew it wouldn't take long. Or suppose the dog seized him by the crotch, instead? Suppose—

But McCarty had said something and was waiting for a response. Pop turned his attention to the man, and any lingering hope he might have held of making a sale evaporated. The Mad Hatter *extraordinaire,* who would cheerfully spend an afternoon with you trying to call up the ghost of your dear departed Uncle Ned, was gone. In his place was McCarty's other side: the hardheaded realist who had made *Fortune* magazine's listing of the richest men in America for twelve straight years—not because he was an airhead who had had the good fortune to inherit both a lot of money and an honest, capable staff to husband and expand it, but because he had been a genius in the field of aerodynamic design and development. He was not as rich as Howard Hughes but not quite as crazy as Hughes had been at the end, either. When it came to psychic phenomena, the man was a Mad Hatter. Outside that one area, however, he was a shark that made the likes of Pop Merrill look like a tadpole swimming in a mud-puddle.

"Sorry," Pop said. "I was woolgatherin a little, Mr. McCarty."

"I said it's fascinating," McCarty said. "Especially the subtle indications of passing time from one photo to the next. How does it work? Camera in camera?"

"I don't understand what you're gettin at."

"No, not a camera," McCarty said, speaking to himself. He picked the camera up and shook it next to his ear. "More likely some sort of roller device."

Pop stared at the man with no idea what he was talking about . . . except it spelled NO SALE, whatever it was. That goddam Christless ride in the little plane (and soon to do over again), all for nothing. But why? *Why?* He had been so *sure* of this fellow, who would probably believe the Brooklyn Bridge was a spectral illusion from the "other side" if you *told* him it was. So *why?*

"Slots, of course!" McCarty said, as delighted as a child. "*Slots!* There's a circular belt on pulleys inside this housing with a number of slots built into it. Each slot contains an exposed Polaroid picture of this dog. Continuity suggests"— he looked carefully at the pictures again—"yes, that the dog might have been *filmed,* with the Polaroids made from individual frames. When the shutter is released, a picture drops from its slot and emerges. The battery turns the belt enough to position the next photo, and—*voilà!*"

His pleasant expression was suddenly gone, and Pop saw a man who looked like he might have made his way to fame and fortune over the broken, bleeding bodies of his competitors . . . and enjoyed it.

"Joe will fly you back," he said. His voice had gone chill and impersonal. "You're good, Mr. Merrill"—this man, Pop realized glumly, would never call him Pop again—"I'll admit that. You've finally overstepped yourself, but for a long time you had me fooled. How much did you take me for? Was it all claptrap?"

"I didn't take you for one red cent," Pop said, lying stoutly. "I never sold you one single thing I didn't b'lieve was the genuine article, and what I mean to say is that goes for that camera as well."

"You make me sick," McCarty said. "Not because I trusted you; I've trusted others who were fakes and shams. Not because you took my money; it wasn't enough to matter. You make me sick because it's men like you that have kept the scientific investigation of psychic phenomena in the dark ages, something to be laughed at, something to be dismissed as the sole province of crackpots and dimwits. The one consolation is that sooner or later you fellows always overstep yourselves. You get greedy and try to palm off something ridiculous like *this*. I want you out of here, Mr. Merrill."

Pop had his pipe in his mouth and a Diamond Blue Tip in one shaking hand. McCarty pointed at him, and the chilly eyes above that finger made it look like the barrel of a gun.

"And if you light that stinking thing in here," he said, "I'll have Joe yank it out of your mouth and dump the coals down the back of your pants. So unless you want to leave my house with your skinny ass in flames, I suggest—"

"What's the *matter* with you, Mr. McCarty?" Pop bleated. "These pitchers didn't come out all developed! *You watched em develop with your own eyes!*"

"An emulsion any kid with a twelve-dollar chemistry set could whip up," McCarty said coldly. "It's not the catalyst-fixative the Polaroid people use, but it's close. You expose your Polaroids—or create them from movie-film, if that's what you did—and then you take them in a standard darkroom and paint them with goop. When they're dry, you load them. When they pop out, they look like any Polaroid that hasn't started to develop yet. Solid gray in a white border. Then the light hits your home-made emulsion, creating a chemical change, and it

97

evaporates, showing a picture you yourself took hours or days or weeks before. Joe?"

Before Pop could say anything else, his arms were seized and he was not so much walked as propelled from the spacious, glass-walled living room. He wouldn't have said anything, anyway. Another of the many things a good businessman had to know was when he was licked. And yet he wanted to shout over his shoulder: *Some dumb cunt with dyed hair and a crystal ball she ordered from* Fate *magazine floats a book or a lamp or a page of goddam sheet-music through a dark room and you bout shit yourself, but when I show you a camera that takes pitchers of some other world, you have me thrown out by the seat of m'pants! You're mad as a hatter, all right! Well, fuck ya! There's other fish in the sea!*

So there were.

On October 5th, Pop got into his perfectly maintained car and drove to Portland to pay a visit on the Pus Sisters.

The Pus Sisters were identical twins who lived in Portland. They were eighty or so but looked older than Stonehenge. They chain-smoked Camel cigarettes, and had done so since they were seventeen, they were happy to tell you. They never coughed in spite of the six packs they smoked between them each and every day. They were driven about—on those rare occasions when they left their red brick Colonial mansion—in a 1958 Lincoln Continental which had the somber glow of a hearse. This vehicle was piloted by a black woman only a little younger than the Pus Sisters themselves. This female chauffeur was probably a mute, but might just be something a bit more special: one of the few truly taciturn human beings God ever made. Pop did not know and had never asked. He had dealt with the two old ladies for nearly thirty years, the black woman had been with them all that time, mostly driving the car, sometimes washing it, sometimes mowing the lawn or clipping the hedges around the house, sometimes stalking down to the mailbox on the corner with letters from the Pus Sisters to God alone knew who (he didn't know if the black woman ever went or was allowed inside the house, either, only that he had never seen her there), and during all that time he had never heard this marvellous creature speak.

The Colonial mansion was in Portland's Bramhall district, which is to Portland what the Beacon Hill area is to Boston. In that latter city, in the land of the bean and the cod, it's said the Cabots speak only to Lowells and the Lowells speak only to God, but the Pus Sisters and their few remaining contemporaries in Portland would and did calmly assert that the Lowells had turned a private connection into a party line some years after the Deeres and their Portland contemporaries had set up the original wire.

And of course no one in his right mind would have called them the Pus Sisters to their identical faces any more than anyone in his right mind would have stuck his nose in a bandsaw to take care of a troublesome itch. They were the Pus Sisters when they weren't around (and when one was fairly sure one was in company which didn't contain a tale-bearer or two), but their real names were Miss Eleusippus Deere and Mrs. Meleusippus Verrill. Their father, in his determination to combine devout Christianity with an exhibition of his own erudition, had named them for two of three triplets who had all become saints . . . but who, unfortunately, had been *male* saints.

Meleusippus's husband had died a great many years before, during the Battle of Leyte Gulf in 1944, as a matter of fact, but she had resolutely kept his name ever since, which made it impossible to take the easy way out and simply call them the Misses Deere. No; you had to practice those goddamned tongue-twister names until they came out as smooth as shit from a waxed asshole. If you fucked up once, they held it against you, and you might lose their custom for as long as six months or a year. Fuck up twice, and don't even bother to call. Ever again.

Pop drove with the steel box containing the Polaroid camera on the seat beside him, saying their names over and over again in a low voice: "Eleusippus. Meleusippus. Eleusippus and Meleusippus. Ayuh. *That's* all right."

But, as it turned out, that was the only thing that *was* all right. They wanted the Polaroid no more than McCarty had wanted it . . . although Pop had been so shaken by *that* encounter he went in fully prepared to take ten thousand dollars less, or fifty per cent of his original confident estimate of what the camera might fetch.

The elderly black woman was raking leaves, revealing a lawn which, October or not, was still as green as the felt on a billiard table. Pop nodded to her. She looked at him, looked *through* him, and continued raking leaves. Pop rang the bell and, somewhere in the depths of the house, a bell bonged. *Mansion* seemed the perfectly proper word for the Pus Sisters' domicile. Although it was nowhere near as big as some of the old homes in the Bramhall district, the perpetual dimness which reigned inside made it seem much bigger. The sound of the bell really *did* seem to come floating through a depth of rooms and corridors, and the sound of that bell always stirred a specific image in Pop's mind: the dead-cart passing through the streets of London during the plague year, the driver ceaselessly tolling his bell and crying, "Bring outcher dead! Bring outcher dead! For the luvva Jaysus, bring outcher dead!"

The Pus Sister who opened the door some thirty seconds later looked not only dead but embalmed; a mummy between whose lips someone had poked the smouldering butt of a cigarette for a joke.

"Merrill," the lady said. Her dress was a deep blue, her hair colored to match. She tried to speak to him as a great lady would speak to a tradesman who had come to the wrong door by mistake, but Pop could see she was, in her way, every bit as excited as that son of a bitch McCarty had been; it was just that the Pus Sisters had been born in Maine, raised in Maine, and would die in Maine, while McCarty hailed from someplace in the Midwest, where the art and craft of taciturnity were apparently not considered an important part of a child's upbringing.

A shadow flitted somewhere near the parlor end of the hallway, just visible over the bony shoulder of the sister who had opened the door. The other one. Oh, they were eager, all right. Pop began to wonder if he couldn't squeeze twelve grand out of them after all. Maybe even fourteen.

Pop knew he *could* say, "Do I have the honor of addressing Miss Deere or Mrs. Verrill?" and be completely correct and completely polite, but he had dealt with this pair of eccentric old bags before and he knew that, while the Pus Sister who had opened the door wouldn't raise an eyebrow or flare a nostril, would simply tell him which one he was speaking to, he would lose at least a thousand by doing so. They took great pride in their odd masculine names, and were apt to look more kindly on a person who tried and failed than one who took the coward's way out.

So, saying a quick mental prayer that his tongue wouldn't fail him now that the moment had come, he gave it his best and was pleased to hear the names slip as smoothly from his tongue as a pitch from a snake-oil salesman: "Is it Eleusippus or Meleusippus?" he asked, his face suggesting he was no more concerned about getting the names right than if they had been Joan and Kate.

"Meleusippus, Mr. Merrill," she said, ah, good, now he was *Mister* Merrill, and he was sure everything was going to go just as slick as ever a man could want, and he was just as wrong as ever a man could be. "Won't you step in?"

"Thank you kindly," Pop said, and entered the gloomy depths of the Deere Mansion.

"Oh *dear*," Eleusippus Deere said as the Polaroid began to develop.

"What a *brute* he looks!" Meleusippus Verrill said, speaking in tones of genuine dismay and fear.

The dog *was* getting uglier, Pop had to admit that, and

there was something else that worried him even more: the time-sequence of the pictures seemed to be speeding up.

He had posed the Pus Sisters on their Queen Anne sofa for the demonstration picture. The camera flashed its bright white light, turning the room for one single instant from the purgatorial zone between the land of the living and that of the dead where these two old relics somehow existed into something flat and tawdry, like a police photo of a museum in which a crime had been committed.

Except the picture which emerged did not show the Pus Sisters sitting together on their parlor sofa like identical bookends. The picture showed the black dog, now turned so that it was full-face to the camera and whatever photographer it was who was nuts enough to stand there and keep snapping pictures of it. Now all of its teeth were exposed in a crazy, homicidal snarl, and its head had taken on a slight, predatory tilt to the left. That head, Pop thought, would continue to tilt as it sprang at its victim, accomplishing two purposes: concealing the vulnerable area of its neck from possible attack and putting the head in a position where, once the teeth were clamped solidly in flesh, it could revolve upright again, ripping a large chunk of living tissue from its target.

"It's so *awful!*" Eleusippus said, putting one mummified hand to the scaly flesh of her neck.

"So *terrible!*" Meleusippus nearly moaned, lighting a fresh Camel from the butt of an old one with a hand shaking so badly she came close to branding the cracked and fissured left corner of her mouth.

"It's totally in-ex-*PLICK*-able!" Pop said triumphantly, thinking: *I wish you was here, McCarty, you happy asshole. I just wish you was. Here's two ladies been round the Horn and back a few times that don't think this goddam camera's just some kind of a carny magic-show trick!*

"Does it show something which *has* happened?" Meleusippus whispered.

"Or something which *will* happen?" Eleusippus added in an equally awed whisper.

"I dunno," Pop said. "All I know for sure is that I have seen some goldarn strange things in my time, but I've never seen the beat of these pitchers."

"I'm not surprised!" Eleusippus.

"Nor I!" Meleusippus.

Pop was all set to start the conversation going in the direction of price—a delicate business when you were dealing with *anyone,* but never more so than when you were dealing with the Pus Sisters: when it got down to hard trading, they were as delicate as a pair of virgins—which, for all Pop knew, at least one of them was. He was just deciding on the *To start with, it never crossed my mind to sell something like this, but* . . . approach (it was older than the Pus Sisters themselves—although probably not by much, you would have said after a good close look at them—but when you were dealing with Mad Hatters, that didn't matter a bit; in fact, they *liked* to hear it, the way small children like to hear the same fairy tales over and over) when Eleusippus absolutely floored him by saying, "I don't know about my sister, Mr. Merrill, but I wouldn't feel comfortable looking at anything you might have to"—here a slight, pained pause—"offer us in a business way until you put that . . . that camera, or whatever God-awful thing it is . . . back in your car."

"I couldn't agree more," Meleusippus said, stubbing out her half-smoked Camel in a fish-shaped ashtray which was doing everything but *shitting* Camel cigarette butts.

"*Ghost* photographs," Eleusippus said, "are one thing. They have a certain—"

"*Dignity,*" Meleusippus suggested.

"Yes! Dignity! But that *dog*—" The old woman actually shivered. "It looks as if it's ready to jump right out of that photograph and *bite* one of us."

"*All* of us!" Meleusippus elaborated.

Up until this last exchange, Pop had been convinced—

perhaps because he *had* to be—that the sisters had merely begun their own part of the dickering, and in admirable style. But the tone of their voices, as identical as their faces and figures (if they could have been said to *have* such things as figures), was beyond his power to disbelieve. They had no doubt that the Sun 660 was exhibiting some sort of paranormal behavior . . . *too* paranormal to suit them. They weren't dickering; they weren't pretending; they weren't playing games with him in an effort to knock the price down. When they said they wanted no part of the camera and the weird thing it was doing, that was exactly what they meant—nor had they done him the discourtesy (and that's just what it would have been, in their minds) of supposing or even *dreaming* that selling it had been his purpose in coming.

Pop looked around the parlor. It was like the old lady's room in a horror movie he'd watched once on his VCR—a piece of claptrap called *Burnt Offerings,* where this big old beefy fella tried to drown his son in the swimming pool but nobody even took their clothes off. That lady's room had been filled, over-filled, actually *stuffed* with old and new photographs. They sat on the tables and the mantel in every sort of frame; they covered so much of the walls you couldn't even tell what the pattern on the frigging paper was supposed to be.

The Pus Sisters' parlor wasn't quite that bad, but there were still plenty of photographs; maybe as many as a hundred and fifty, which seemed like three times that many in a room as small and dim as this one. Pop had been here often enough to notice most of them at least in passing, and he knew others even better than that, for he had been the one to sell them to Eleusippus and Meleusippus.

They had a great many more "ghost photographs," as Eleusippus Deere called them, perhaps as many as a thousand in all, but apparently even they had realized a room the size of their parlor was limited in terms of display-space, if not in those of taste. The rest of the ghost photographs were distributed among the mansion's other fourteen rooms. Pop had seen them all. He was one of the fortunate few who had been granted what the Pus Sisters called, with simple grandiosity, The Tour. But it was here in the parlor that they kept their *prize* "ghost photographs," with the prize of prizes attracting the eye by the simple fact that it stood in solitary splendor atop the closed Steinway baby grand by the bow windows. In it, a corpse was levitating from its coffin before fifty or sixty horrified mourners. It was a fake, of course. A child of ten— hell, a child of *eight*—would have known it was a fake. It made the photographs of the dancing elves which had so bewitched poor Arthur Conan Doyle near the end of his life look accomplished by comparison. In fact, as Pop ranged his eye about the room, he saw only two photographs that weren't obvious fakes. It would take closer study to see how the trickery had been worked in those. Yet these two ancient pussies, who had collected "ghost photographs" all their lives and claimed to be great experts in the field, acted like a couple of teenage girls at a horror movie when he showed them not just a paranormal *photograph* but a goddam Jesus-jumping paranormal *camera* that didn't just do its trick once and then quit, like the one that had taken the picture of the ghost-lady watching the fox-hunters come home, but one that did it *again* and *again* and *again,* and how much had they spent on this stuff that was nothing but *claptrap?* Thousands? Tens of thousands? *Hundreds* of—

"—show us?" Meleusippus was asking him.

Pop Merrill forced his lips to turn up in what must have been at least a reasonable imitation of his Folksy Crackerbarrel Smile, because they registered no surprise or distrust.

"Pardon me, dear lady," Pop said. "M'mind went woolgatherin all on its own for a minute or two there. I guess it happens to all of us as we get on."

"We're eighty-three, and *our* minds are as clear as window-glass," Eleusippus said with clear disapproval.

"*Freshly washed* window-glass," Meleusippus added. "I asked if you have some new photographs you would care to show us . . . once you've put that wretched thing away, of course."

"It's been *ages* since we saw any really *good* new ones," Eleusippus said, lighting a fresh Camel.

"We went to The New England Psychic and Tarot Convention in Providence last month," Meleusippus said, "and while the lectures were enlightening—"

"—and uplifting—"

"—so many of the photographs were *arrant* fakes! Even a child of ten—"

"—of *seven!*—"

"—could have seen through them. So . . ." Meleusippus paused. Her face assumed an expression of perplexity which looked as if it might hurt (the muscles of her face having long since atrophied into expressions of mild pleasure and serene knowledge). "I am puzzled. Mr. Merrill, I must admit to being a bit puzzled."

"I was about to say the same thing," Eleusippus said.

"Why *did* you bring that awful thing?" Meleusippus and Eleusippus asked in perfect two-part harmony, spoiled only by the nicotine rasp of their voices.

The urge Pop felt to say *Because I didn't know what a pair of chickenshit old cunts you two were* was so strong that for one horrified second he believed he *had* said it, and he quailed, waiting for the twin screams of outrage to rise in the dim and hallowed confines of the parlor, screams which would rise like the squeal of rusty bandsaws biting into tough pine-knots, and go on rising until the glass in the frame of every bogus picture in the room shattered in an agony of vibration.

The idea that he had spoken such a terrible thought aloud lasted only a split-second, but when he relived it on later wakeful nights while the clocks rustled sleepily below (and while Kevin Delevan's Polaroid crouched sleeplessly in the locked drawer of the worktable), it seemed much longer. In those sleepless hours, he sometimes found himself wishing he *had* said it, and wondered if he was maybe losing his mind.

What he *did* do was react with a speed and a canny instinct for self-preservation that were nearly noble. To blow up at the Pus Sisters would give him immense gratification, but it would, unfortunately, be *short-lived* gratification. If he buttered them up—which was exactly what they expected, since they had been basted in butter all their lives (although it hadn't done a goddam thing for their skins)—he could perhaps sell them another three or four thousand dollars' worth of clap-trap "ghost photographs," if they continued to elude the lung cancer which should surely have claimed one or both at least a dozen years ago.

And there were, after all, other Mad Hatters in Pop's mental file, although not quite so many as he'd thought on the day he'd set off to see Cedric McCarty. A little checking had revealed that two had died and one was currently learning how to weave baskets in a posh northern California retreat which catered to the incredibly rich who also happened to have gone hopelessly insane.

"Actually," he said, "I brought the camera out so you ladies could look at it. What I mean to say," he hastened on, observing their expressions of consternation, "is I know how much experience you ladies have in this field."

Consternation turned to gratification; the sisters exchanged smug, comfy looks, and Pop found himself wishing he could douse a couple of their goddam packs of Camels with barbecue lighter fluid and jam them up their tight little old-maid asses and then strike a match. They'd smoke then, all right. They'd smoke just like plugged chimneys, was what he meant to say.

"I thought you might have some advice on what I should do with the camera, is what I mean to say," he finished.

"Destroy it," Eleusippus said immediately.

"I'd use dynamite," Meleusippus said.

"Acid first, *then* dynamite," Eleusippus said.

"Right," Meleusippus finished. "It's dangerous. You don't have to look at that devil-dog to know that." She did look

107

though; they both did, and identical expressions of revulsion and fear crossed their faces.

"You can feel *eeevil* coming out of it," Eleusippus said in a voice of such portentousness that it should have been laughable, like a high-school girl playing a witch in *Macbeth,* but which somehow wasn't. "Destroy it, Mr. Merrill. Before something awful happens. Before—perhaps, you'll notice I only say *perhaps*—it destroys *you.*"

"Now, now," Pop said, annoyed to find he felt just a little uneasy in spite of himself, "that's drawing it a little strong. It's just a camera, is what I mean to say."

Eleusippus Deere said quietly: "And the planchette that put out poor Colette Simineaux's eye a few years ago—that was nothing but a piece of fiberboard."

"At least until those foolish, foolish, *foolish* people put their fingers on it and woke it up," Meleusippus said, more quietly still.

There seemed nothing left to say. Pop picked up the camera—careful to do so by the strap, not touching the actual camera itself, although he told himself this was just for the benefit of these two old pussies—and stood.

"Well, you're the experts," he said. The two old women looked at each other and preened.

Yes; retreat. Retreat was the answer . . . for now, at least. But he wasn't done yet. Every dog had its day, and you could take *that* to the bank. "I don't want to take up any more of y'time, and I surely don't want to discommode you."

"Oh, you haven't!" Eleusippus said, also rising.

"We have so very few guests these days!" Meleusippus said, also rising.

"Put it in your car, Mr. Merrill," Eleusippus said, "and then—"

"—come in and have tea."

"*High* tea!"

And although Pop wanted nothing more in his life than to be *out* of there (and to tell them exactly that: *Thanks but no thanks, I want to get the fuck OUT of here)*, he made a courtly little half-bow and an excuse of the same sort. "It would be my pleasure," he said, "but I'm afraid I have another appointment. I don't get to the city as often as I'd like." If you're going to tell one lie, you might as well tell a pack, Pop's own Pop had often told him, and it was advice he had taken to heart. He made a business of looking at his watch. "I've stayed too long already. You girls have made me late, I'm afraid, but I suppose I'm not the first man you've done *that* to."

They giggled and actually raised identical blushes, like the glow of very old roses. "Why, Mr. *Merrill!*" Eleusippus trilled.

"Ask me next time," he said, smiling until his face felt as if it would break. "Ask me next time, by the Lord Harry! You just ask and see if I don't say yes faster'n a hoss can trot!"

He went out, and as one of them quickly closed the door behind him (maybe they think the sun'll fade their goddam fake ghost photographs, Pop thought sourly), he turned and snapped the Polaroid at the old black woman, who was still raking leaves. He did it on impulse, as a man with a mean streak may on impulse swerve across a country road to kill a skunk or raccoon.

The black woman's upper lip rose in a snarl, and Pop was stunned to see she was actually forking the sign of the evil eye at him.

He got into his car and backed hurriedly down the driveway.

The rear end of his car was halfway into the street and he was turning to check for traffic when his eye happened upon the Polaroid he had just taken. It wasn't fully developed; it had the listless, milky look of all Polaroid photographs which are still developing.

Yet it had come up enough so that Pop only stared at it, the breath he had begun to unthinkingly draw into his lungs suddenly ceasing like a breeze that unaccountably drops away to nothing for a moment. His very heart seemed to cease in mid-beat.

What Kevin had imagined was now happening. The dog had finished its pivot, and had now begun its relentless ordained irrefutable approach toward the camera and whoever held it . . . ah, but *he* had held it this time, hadn't he? *He,* Reginald Marion "Pop" Merrill, had raised it and snapped it at the old black woman in a moment's pique like a spanked child that shoots a pop bottle off the top of a fence-post with his BB gun because he can't very well shoot his father, although in that humiliating, bottom-throbbing time directly after the paddling he would be more than happy to.

The dog was coming. Kevin had known that would happen next, and Pop would have known it, too, if he'd had occasion to think on it, which he hadn't—although from this moment on he would find it hard to think of anything else when he thought of the camera, and he would find those thoughts filling more and more of his time, both waking and dreaming.

It's coming, Pop thought with the sort of frozen horror a man might feel standing in the dark as some Thing, some unspeakable and unbearable Thing, approaches with its razor-sharp claws and teeth. *Oh my God, it's coming, that dog is coming.*

But it wasn't just *coming;* it was *changing.*

It was impossible to say how. His eyes hurt, caught between what they should be seeing and what they *were* seeing, and in the end the only handle he could find was a very small one: it was as if someone had changed the lens on the camera, from the normal one to a fish-eye, so that the dog's forehead with its clots of tangled fur seemed somehow to bulge and recede at the same time, and the dog's murderous eyes seemed to have taken on filthy, barely visible glimmers of red, like the sparks a Polaroid flash sometimes puts in people's eyes.

The dog's *body* seemed to have elongated but not thinned; if anything, it seemed thicker—not fatter, but more heavily muscled.

And its teeth were bigger. Longer. Sharper.

Pop suddenly found himself remembering Joe Camber's

Saint Bernard, Cujo—the one who had killed Joe and that old tosspot Gary Pervier and Big George Bannerman. The dog had gone rabid. It had trapped a woman and a young boy in their car up there at Camber's place and after two or three days the kid had died. And now Pop found himself wondering if *this* was what they had been looking at during those long days and nights trapped in the steaming oven of their car; this or something like this, the muddy red eyes, the long sharp teeth—

A horn blared impatiently.

Pop screamed, his heart not only starting again but *gunning,* like the engine of a Formula One racing-car.

A van swerved around his sedan, still half in the driveway and half in the narrow residential street. The van's driver stuck his fist out his open window and his middle finger popped up.

"Eat my dick, you son of a whore!" Pop screamed. He backed the rest of the way out, but so jerkily that he bumped up over the curb on the far side of the street. He twisted the wheel viciously (inadvertently honking his horn in the process) and then drove off. But three blocks south he had to pull over and just sit there behind the wheel for ten minutes, waiting for the shakes to subside enough so he could drive.

So much for the Pus Sisters.

During the next five days, Pop ran through the remaining names on his mental list. His asking price, which had begun at twenty thousand dollars with McCarty and dropped to ten with the Pus Sisters (not that he had gotten far enough into the business to mention price in either case), dropped steadily as he ran out the string. He was finally left with Emory Chaffee, and the possibility of realizing perhaps twenty-five hundred.

Chaffee presented a fascinating paradox: in all Pop's experience with the Mad Hatters—an experience that was long and amazingly varied—Emory Chaffee was the only believer in the "other world" who had absolutely no imagination whatsoever.

That he had ever spared a single thought for the "other world" with such a mind was surprising; that he *believed* in it was amazing; that he paid good money to collect objects connected with it was something Pop found absolutely astounding. Yet it was so, and Pop would have put Chaffee much higher on his list save for the annoying fact that Chaffee was by far the least well off of what Pop thought of as his "rich" Mad Hatters. He was doing a game but poor job of holding onto the last unravelling threads of what had once been a great family fortune. Hence, another large drop in Pop's asking price for Kevin's Polaroid.

But, he had thought, pulling his car into the overgrown driveway of what had in the '20s been one of Sebago Lake's finest summer homes and which was now only a step or two away from becoming one of Sebago Lake's shabbiest year-round homes (the Chaffee house in Portland's Bramhall district had been sold for taxes fifteen years before), *if anyone'll buy this beshitted thing, I reckon Emory will.*

The only thing that really distressed him—and it had done so more and more as he worked his way fruitlessly down the list—was the demonstration part. He could *describe* what the camera did until he was black in the face, but not even an odd duck like Emory Chaffee would lay out good money on the basis of a description alone.

Sometimes Pop thought it had been stupid to have Kevin take all those pictures so he could make that videotape. But when you got right down to where the bear shit in the buckwheat, he wasn't sure it would have made any difference. Time passed over there in that world (for, like Kevin, he had come to think of it as that: an actual world), and it passed much more slowly than it did in this one . . . but wasn't it speeding up as the dog approached the camera? Pop thought it was. The movement of the dog along the fence had been barely visible at first; now only a blind man could fail to see that the dog was closer each time the shutter was pressed. You could see the difference in distance even if you snapped two photographs one right after the other. It was almost as if time over there were trying to . . . well, trying to *catch up* somehow, and get in sync with time over here.

If that had been all, it would have been bad enough. But it *wasn't* all.

That was no *dog,* goddammit.

Pop didn't know what it *was,* but he knew as well as he knew his mother was buried in Homeland Cemetery that it was no *dog.*

He thought it *had* been a dog, when it had been snuffling its way along that picket fence which it had now left a good ten feet behind; it had *looked* like one, albeit an exceptionally mean one once it got its head turned enough so you could get a good look at its phiz.

But to Pop it now looked like no creature that had ever existed on God's earth, and probably not in Lucifer's hell, either. What troubled him even more was this: the few people for whom he had taken demonstration photographs did not seem to see this. They inevitably recoiled, inevitably said it was the ugliest, meanest-looking junkyard mongrel they had ever seen, but that was all. Not a single one of them suggested that the dog in Kevin's Sun 660 was turning into some kind of monster as it approached the photographer. As it approached the lens which might be some sort of portal between that world and this one.

Pop thought again (as Kevin had), *But it could never get through. Never. If something is going to happen, I'll tell you what that something will be, because that thing is an* ANIMAL, *maybe a goddam ugly one, a scary one, even, like the kind of thing a little kid imagines in his closet after his momma turns off the lights, but it's still an* ANIMAL, *and if anything happens it'll be this: there'll be one last pitcher where you can't see nothing but blur because that devil-dog will have jumped, you can see that's what it means to do, and after that the camera either won't work, or if it does, it won't take pitchers that develop into anything but black squares, because you can't take pitchers with a camera that has a busted lens or with one that's broke right in two for that matter, and if whoever owns that shadow drops the camera when the devil-dog hits it and him, and I imagine he will, it's apt to fall on the sidewalk and it probably WILL break. Goddam thing's nothing but plastic, after all, and plastic and cement don't get along hardly at all.*

But Emory Chaffee had come out on his splintery porch now, where the paint on the boards was flaking off and the boards themselves were warping out of true and the screens were turning the rusty color of dried blood and gaping holes in some of them; Emory Chaffee wearing a blazer which had once been a natty blue but had now been cleaned so many times it was the nondescript gray of an elevator operator's uniform; Emory Chaffee with his high forehead sloping back and back until it finally disappeared beneath what little hair he had left and grinning his *Pip-pip, jolly good, old boy, jolly good, wot, wot?* grin that showed his gigantic buck teeth and made him look the way Pop imagined Bugs Bunny would look if Bugs had suffered some cataclysmic mental retardation.

Pop took hold of the camera's strap—God, how he had come to hate the thing!—got out of his car, and forced himself to return the man's wave and grin.

Business, after all, was business.

"That's one ugly pup, wouldn't you say?"

Chaffee was studying the Polaroid which was now almost completely developed. Pop had explained what the camera did, and had been encouraged by Chaffee's frank interest and curiosity. Then he had given the Sun to the man, inviting him to take a picture of anything he liked.

Emory Chaffee, grinning that repulsive buck-toothed grin, swung the Polaroid Pop's way.

"Except me," Pop said hastily. "I'd ruther you pointed a shotgun at my head instead of that camera."

"When you sell a thing, you really sell it," Chaffee said

admiringly, but he had obliged just the same, turning the Sun 660 toward the wide picture window with its view of the lake, a magnificent view that remained as rich now as the Chaffee family itself had been in those years which began after World War I, golden years which had somehow begun to turn to brass around 1970.

He pressed the shutter.

The camera whined.

Pop winced. He found that now he winced every time he heard that sound—that squidgy little whine. He had tried to control the wince and had found to his dismay that he could not.

"Yes, sir, one goddamned ugly brute!" Chaffee repeated after examining the developed picture, and Pop was sourly pleased to see that the repulsive buck-toothed wot-ho, bit-of-a-sticky-wicket grin had disappeared at last. The camera had been able to do that much, at least.

Yet it was equally clear to him that the man wasn't seeing what he, Pop, was seeing. Pop had had some preparation for this eventuality; he was, all the same, badly shaken behind his impassive Yankee mask. He believed that if Chaffee *had* been granted the power (for that was what it seemed to be) to see what Pop was seeing, the stupid fuck would have been headed for the nearest door, and at top speed.

The dog—well, it wasn't a dog, not anymore, but you had to call it *something*—hadn't begun its leap at the photographer yet, but it was getting ready; its hindquarters were simultaneously bunching and lowering toward the cracked anonymous sidewalk in a way that somehow reminded Pop of a kid's souped-up car, trembling, barely leashed by the clutch during the last few seconds of a red light; the needle on the rpm dial already standing straight up at 60×10, the engine screaming through chrome pipes, fat deep-tread tires ready to smoke the macadam in a hot soul-kiss.

The dog's face was no longer a recognizable thing at all. It had twisted and distorted into a carny freak-show thing that seemed to have but a single dark and malevolent eye, neither round nor oval but somehow *runny,* like the yolk of an egg that has been stabbed with the tines of a fork. Its nose was a black beak with deep flared holes drilled into either side. And was there *smoke* coming from those holes—like steam from the vents of a volcano? Maybe—or maybe that part was just imagination.

Don't matter, Pop thought. *You just keep workin that shutter, or lettin people like this fool work it, and you are gonna find out, aren't you?*

But he didn't *want* to find out. He looked at the black, murdering thing whose matted coat had caught perhaps two dozen wayward burdocks, the thing which no longer had fur, exactly, but stuff like living spikes, and a tail like a medieval weapon. He observed the shadow it had taken a damned snot-nosed kid to extract meaning from, and saw it had changed. One of the shadow-legs appeared to have moved a stride backward—a very *long* stride, even taking the effect of the lowering or rising sun (but it was going down; Pop had somehow become very sure it was going down, that it was night coming in that world over there, not day) into account.

The photographer over there in that world had finally discovered that his subject did not mean to sit for its portrait; that had never been a part of its plan. It intended to *eat,* not *sit. That* was the plan.

Eat, and, maybe, in some way he didn't understand, escape.

Find out! he thought ironically. *Go ahead! Just keep taking pitchers! You'll find out! You'll find out* PLENTY!

"And you, sir," Emory Chaffee was saying, for he had only been stopped for a moment; creatures of little imagination are rarely stopped for long by such trivial things as consideration, "are one hell of a salesman!"

The memory of McCarty was still very close to the surface of Pop's mind, and it still rankled.

"If you think it's a fake—" he began.

"A fake? Not at all! Not . . . at *all!*" Chaffee's buck-toothed smile spread wide in all its repulsive splendor. He spread his hands in a surely-you-jest motion. "But I'm afraid, you see, that we can't do business on this particular item, Mr. Merrill. I'm sorry to say so, but—"

"Why?" Pop bit off. "If you don't think the goddam thing's a fake, why in the hell don't you want it?" And he was astonished to hear his voice rising in a kind of plaintive, balked fury. There had never been anything like this, never in the history of the *world,* Pop was sure of it, nor ever would be again. Yet it seemed he couldn't *give* the goddam thing away.

"But . . ." Chaffee looked puzzled, as if not sure how to state it, because whatever it was he had to say seemed so obvious to him. In that moment he looked like a pleasant but not very capable pre-school teacher trying to teach a backward child how to tie his shoes. "But it doesn't *do* anything, does it?"

"Doesn't *do* anything?" Pop nearly screamed. He couldn't believe he had lost control of himself to such a degree as this, and was losing more all the time. What was happening to him? Or, cutting closer to the bone, what was the son-of-a-bitching *camera* doing to him? "Doesn't *do* anything? What are you, blind? It takes pitchers of *another world!* It takes pitchers that move in time from one to the next, no matter *where* you take em or *when* you take em in *this* world! And that . . . that thing . . . that *monster*—"

Oh. Oh dear. He had finally done it. He had finally gone too far. He could see it in the way Chaffee was looking at him.

"But it's just a dog, isn't it?" Chaffee said in a low, comforting voice. It was the sort of voice you'd use to try and soothe a madman while the nurses ran for the cabinet where they kept the hypos and the knock-out stuff.

"Ayuh," Pop said slowly and tiredly. "Just a dog is all it is. But you said yourself it was a hell of an ugly brute."

"That's right, that's right, I did," Chaffee said, agreeing much too quickly. Pop thought if the man's grin got any

117

wider and broader he might just be treated to the sight of the top three-quarters of the idiot's head toppling off into his lap. "But . . . surely you see, Mr. Merrill . . . what a problem this presents for the collector. The *serious* collector."

"No, I guess I don't," Pop said, but after running through the entire list of Mad Hatters, a list which had seemed so promising at first, he was beginning to. In fact, he was beginning to see a whole *host* of problems the Polaroid Sun presented for the serious collector. As for Emory Chaffee . . . God knew what Emory thought, exactly.

"There are most certainly such things as ghost photographs," Chaffee said in a rich, pedantic voice that made Pop want to strangle him. "But these are not ghost photographs. They—"

"They're sure as hell not *normal* photographs!"

"My point exactly," Chaffee said, frowning slightly. "But what sort of photographs *are* they? One can hardly say, can one? One can only display a perfectly normal camera that photographs a dog which is apparently preparing to leap. And once it leaps, it will be gone from the frame of the picture. At that point, one of three things may happen. The camera may start taking normal pictures, which is to say, pictures of the things it is aimed at; it may take no more pictures at all, its one purpose, to photograph—to *document,* one might even say—that dog, completed; or it may simply go on taking pictures of that white fence and the ill-tended lawn behind it." He paused and added, "I suppose someone might walk by at some point, forty photographs down the line—or four hundred—but unless the photographer raised his angle, which he doesn't seem to have done in any of these, one would only see the passerby from the waist down. More or less." And, echoing Kevin's father without even knowing who Kevin's father was, he added: "Pardon me for saying so, Mr. Merrill, but you've shown me something I thought I'd never see: an inexplicable and almost irrefutable paranormal occurrence that is really quite boring."

This amazing but apparently sincere remark forced Pop to disregard whatever Chaffee might think about his sanity and ask again: "It really *is* only a dog, as far as you can see?"

"Of course," Chaffee said, looking mildly surprised. "A stray mongrel that looks exceedingly bad-tempered."

He sighed.

"And it wouldn't be taken seriously, of course. What I mean is it wouldn't be taken seriously by people who don't know you personally, Mr. Merrill. People who aren't familiar with your honesty and reliability in these matters. It looks like a trick, you see? And not even a very good one. Something on the order of a child's Magic Eight-Ball."

Two weeks ago, Pop would have argued strenuously against such an idea. But that was before he had been not walked but actually *propelled* from that bastard McCarty's house.

"Well, if that's your final word," Pop said, getting up and taking the camera by the strap.

"I'm very sorry you made a trip to such little purpose," Chaffee said . . . and then his horrid grin burst forth again, all rubbery lips and huge teeth shining with spit. "I was about to make myself a Spam sandwich when you drove in. Would you care to join me, Mr. Merrill? I make quite a nice one, if I do say so myself. I add a little horseradish and Bermuda onion— that's my secret—and then I—"

"I'll pass," Pop said heavily. As in the Pus Sisters' parlor, all he really wanted right now was to get out of here and put miles between himself and this grinning idiot. Pop had a definite allergy to places where he had gambled and lost. Just lately there seemed to be a lot of those. Too goddam many. "I already had m'dinner, is what I mean to say. Got to be gettin back."

Chaffee laughed fruitily. "The lot of the toiler in the vine-yards is busy but yields great bounty," he said.

Not just lately, Pop thought. *Just lately it ain't yielded no fuckin bounty at all.*

"It's a livin, anyway," Pop replied, and was eventually

allowed out of the house, which was damp and chill (what it must be like to live in such a place come February, Pop couldn't imagine) and had that mousy, mildewed smell that might be rotting curtains and sofa-covers and such . . . or just the smell money leaves behind when it has spent a longish period of time in a place and then departed. He thought the fresh October air, tinged with just a small taste of the lake and a stronger tang of pine-needles, had never smelled so good.

He got into his car and started it up. Emory Chaffee, unlike the Pus Sister who had shown him as far as the door and then closed it quickly behind him, as if afraid the sun might strike her and turn her to dust like a vampire, was standing on the front porch, grinning his idiot grin and actually *waving,* as if he were seeing Pop off on a goddam ocean cruise.

And, without thinking, just as he had taken the picture of (or *at,* anyway) the old black woman without thinking, he had snapped Chaffee and the just-starting-to-moulder house which was all that remained of the Chaffee family holdings. He didn't remember picking the camera up off the seat where he had tossed it in disgust before closing his door, was not even aware that the camera was in his hands or the shutter fired until he heard the whine of the mechanism shoving the photograph out like a tongue coated with some bland gray fluid—Milk of Magnesia, perhaps. That sound seemed to vibrate along his nerve-endings now, making them scream; it was like the feeling you got when something too cold or hot hit a new filling.

He was peripherally aware that Chaffee was laughing as if it was the best goddam joke in the world before snatching the picture from the slot in a kind of furious horror, telling himself he had imagined the momentary, blurred sound of a snarl, a sound like you might hear if a power-boat was approaching while you had your head ducked under water; telling himself he had imagined the momentary feeling that the camera had *bulged* in his hands, as if some huge pressure inside had pushed the sides out momentarily. He punched the glove-compartment button and threw the picture inside and then closed it so hard and fast that he tore his thumbnail all the way down to the tender quick.

He pulled out jerkily, almost stalling, then almost hitting one of the hoary old spruces which flanked the house end of the long Chaffee driveway, and all the way up that driveway he thought he could hear Emory Chaffee laughing in loud mindless cheery bellows of sound: *Haw! Haw! Haw! Haw!*

His heart slammed in his chest, and his head felt as if someone was using a sledgehammer inside there. The small cluster of veins which nestled in the hollows of each temple pulsed steadily.

He got himself under control little by little. Five miles, and the little man inside his head quit using the sledgehammer. Ten miles (by now he was almost halfway back to Castle Rock), and his heartbeat was back to normal. And he told himself: *You ain't gonna look at it. You AIN'T. Let the goddam thing rot in there. You don't need to look at it, and you don't need to take no more of em, either. Time to mark the thing off as a dead loss. Time to do what you should have let the boy do in the first place.*

So of course when he got to the Castle View rest area, a turnout from which you could, it seemed, see all of western Maine and half of New Hampshire, he swung in and turned off his motor and opened the glove compartment and brought out the picture which he had taken with no more intent or knowledge than a man might have if he did a thing while walking in his sleep. The photograph had developed in there, of course; the chemicals inside that deceptively flat square had come to life and done their usual efficient job. Dark or light, it didn't make any difference to a Polaroid picture.

The dog-thing was crouched all the way down now. It was as fully coiled as it was going to get, a trigger pulled back to full cock. Its teeth had outgrown its mouth so that the thing's snarl seemed now to be not only an expression of rage but a simple necessity; how could its lips ever fully close over those teeth? How could those jaws ever chew? It looked more like a weird species of wild boar than a dog now, but what it really looked like was nothing Pop had ever seen before. It did more than hurt his eyes to look at it; it hurt his *mind.* It made him feel as if he was going crazy.

Why not get rid of that camera right here? he thought suddenly. *You can. Just get out, walk to the guardrail there, and toss her over. All gone. Goodbye.*

But that would have been an impulsive act, and Pop Merrill belonged to the Reasonable tribe—belonged to it body and soul, is what I mean to say. He didn't want to do anything on the spur of the moment that he might regret later, and—

If you don't *do this, you'll regret it later.*

But no. And no. And no. A man couldn't run against his nature. It was unnatural. He needed time to think. To be sure.

He compromised by throwing the print out instead and then drove on quickly. For a minute or two he felt as if he might throw up, but the urge passed. When it did, he felt a little more himself. Safely back in his shop, he unlocked the steel box, took out the Sun, rummaged through his keys once more, and located the one for the drawer where he kept his "special" items. He started to put the camera inside . . . and paused, brow furrowed. The image of the chopping block out back entered his mind with such clarity, every detail crisply limned, that it was like a photograph itself.

He thought: *Never mind all that about how a man can't run against his nature. That's crap, and you know it. It ain't in a man's nature to eat dirt, but you could eat a whole bowl of it, by the bald-headed Christ, if someone with a gun pointed at your head told you to do it. You know what time it is, chummy—time to do what you should have let the boy do in the first place. After all, it ain't like you got any investment in this.*

But at this, another part of his mind rose in angry, fist-waving protest. *Yes I do! I do have an investment, goddammit! That kid smashed a perfectly good Polaroid camera! He may not know it, but that don't change the fact that I'm out a hundred and thirty-nine bucks!*

"Oh, shit on toast!" he muttered agitatedly. "It ain't that! It ain't the fuckin *money!*"

No—it wasn't the fucking money. He could at least admit that it wasn't the money. He could afford it; Pop could indeed have afforded a great deal, including his own mansion in Portland's Bramhall district and a brand-new Mercedes-Benz to go in the carport. He never would have bought those things—he pinched his pennies and chose to regard almost pathological miserliness as nothing more than good old Yankee thrift—but that didn't mean he couldn't have had them if he so chose.

It wasn't about money; it was about something more important than money ever could be. It was about *not getting skinned.* Pop had made a life's work out of *not getting skinned,* and on the few occasions when he had been, he had felt like a man with red ants crawling around inside his skull.

Take the business of the goddam Kraut record-player, for instance. When Pop found out that antique dealer from Boston—Donahue, his name had been—had gotten fifty bucks more than he'd ought to have gotten for a 1915 Victor-Graff gramophone (which had actually turned out to be a much more common 1919 model), Pop had lost three hundred dollars' worth of sleep over it, sometimes plotting various forms of revenge (each more wild-eyed and ridiculous than the last), sometimes just damning himself for a fool, telling himself he must really be slipping if a city man like that Donahue could skin Pop Merrill. And sometimes he imagined the fucker telling his poker-buddies about how easy it had been, hell, they were all just a bunch of rubes up there, he believed that if you tried to sell the Brooklyn Bridge to a fellow like that country mouse Merrill in Castle Rock, the damned fool would ask "How much?" Then him and his cronies rocking back in their chairs around that poker-table (why he always saw them around such a table in this morbid daydream Pop didn't know, but he did), smoking dollar cigars and roaring with laughter like a bunch of trolls.

The business of the Polaroid was eating into him like acid, but he still wasn't ready to let go of the thing yet.

Not quite yet.

You're crazy! a voice shouted at him. *You're crazy to go on with it!*

"Damned if I'll eat it," he muttered sulkily to that voice and to his empty shadowed store, which ticked softly to itself like a bomb in a suitcase. *"Damned* if I will."

But that didn't mean he had to go haring off on any more stupid goddam trips trying to sell the sonofawhore, and he *certainly* didn't mean to take any more pictures with it. He judged there were at least three more "safe" ones left in it, and there were *probably* as many as seven, but he wasn't going to be the one to find out. Not at all.

Still, something might come up. You never knew. And it could hardly do him or anyone else any harm locked up in a drawer, could it?

"Nope," Pop agreed briskly to himself. He dropped the camera inside, locked the drawer, repocketed his keys, and then went to the door and turned CLOSED over to OPEN with the air of a man who has finally put some nagging problem behind him for good.

CHAPTER TEN

Pop woke up at three the next morning, bathed with sweat and peering fearfully into the dark. The clocks had just begun another weary run at the hour.

It was not this sound which awakened him, although it could have done, since he was not upstairs in his bed but down below, in the shop itself. The Emporium Galorium was a cave of darkness crowded with hulking shadows created by the streetlamp outside, which managed to send just enough light through the dirty plate-glass windows to create the unpleasant feeling of things hiding beyond the borders of vision.

It wasn't the *clocks* that woke him; it was the *flash*.

He was horrified to find himself standing in his pajamas beside his worktable with the Polaroid Sun 660 in his hands. The "special" drawer was open. He was aware that, although he had taken only a single picture, his finger had been pushing the button which triggered the shutter again and again and again. He would have taken a great many more than the one that protruded from the slot at the bottom of the camera but for simple good luck. There had only been a single picture left in the film pack currently in the camera.

Pop started to lower his arms—he had been holding the camera pointed toward the front of the shop, the viewfinder with its minute hairline crack held up to one open, sleeping eye—and when he got them down as far as his ribcage, they began to tremble and the muscles holding the hinges of his elbows just seemed to give way. His arms fell, his fingers opened, and the camera tumbled back into the "special" drawer with a clatter. The picture he had taken slipped from the slot and fluttered. It struck one edge of the open drawer, teetered first one way as if it would follow the camera in, and then the other. It fell on the floor.

Heart attack, Pop thought incoherently. *I'm gonna have a goddam Christing heart attack.*

He tried to raise his right arm, wanting to massage the left side of his chest with the hand on the end of it, but the arm wouldn't come. The hand on the end of it dangled as limp as a dead man at the end of a hangrope. The world wavered in and out of focus. The sound of the clocks (the tardy ones were just finishing up) faded away to distant echoes. Then the pain in his chest diminished, the light seemed to come back a little, and he realized all he was doing was trying to faint.

He made to sit down in the wheeled chair behind the worktable, and the business of lowering himself into the seat, like the business of lowering the camera, began all right, but before he had gotten even halfway down, *those* hinges, the ones that strapped his thighs and calves together by way of his knees, also gave way and he didn't so much sit in the chair as cave into it. It rolled a foot backward, struck a crate filled with old *Life* and *Look* magazines, and stopped.

Pop put his head down, the way you were supposed to do when you felt lightheaded, and time passed. He had no idea at all, then or later, how much. He might even have gone back to sleep for a little while. But when he raised his head, he was more or less all right again. There was a steady dull throbbing at his temples and behind his forehead, probably because he had stuffed his goddam noodle with blood, hanging it over so long that way, but he found he could stand up and he knew what he had to do. When the thing had gotten hold of him so badly it could make him walk in his sleep, then make him (his mind tried to revolt at that verb, that *make,* but he wouldn't let it) take pictures with it, that was enough. He had no idea what the goddam thing was, but one thing was clear: you couldn't compromise with it.

Time to do what you should have let the boy do in the first place.

Yes. But not tonight. He was exhausted, drenched with sweat, and shivering. He thought he would have his work cut out for him just climbing the stairs to his apartment again, let alone swinging that sledge. He supposed he could do the job in here, simply pick it out of the drawer and dash it against the floor again and again, but there was a deeper truth, and he'd better own up to it: he couldn't have any more truck with that camera tonight. The morning would be time enough . . . and the camera couldn't do any damage between now and then, could it? There was no film in it.

Pop shut the drawer and locked it. Then he got up slowly, looking more like a man pushing eighty than seventy, and tottered slowly to the stairs. He climbed them one at a time, resting on each, clinging to the bannister (which was none too solid itself) with one hand while he held his heavy bunch of keys on their steel ring in the other. At last he made the top. With the door shut behind him, he seemed to feel a little stronger. He went back into his bedroom and got into bed, unaware as always of the strong yellow smell of sweat and old man that puffed up when he lay down—he changed the sheets on the first of every month and called it good.

I won't sleep now, he thought, and then: *Yes you will. You will because you can, and you can because tomorrow morning you're going to take the sledge and pound that fucking thing to pieces and there's an end to it.*

This thought and sleep came simultaneously, and Pop slept without dreaming, almost without moving, all the rest of that night. When he woke he was astonished to hear the clocks downstairs seeming to chime an extra stroke, all of them: eight instead of seven. It wasn't until he looked at the light falling across the floor and wall in a slightly slanted oblong that he realized it really *was* eight; he had overslept for the first time in ten years. Then he remembered the night before. Now, in daylight, the whole episode seemed less weird; had he nearly

127

fainted? Or was that maybe just a natural sort of weakness that came to a sleepwalker when he was unexpectedly wakened?

But of course, that was it, wasn't it? A little bright morning sunshine wasn't going to change that central fact: he *had* walked in his sleep, he *had* taken at least one picture and would have taken a whole slew of them if there had been more film in the pack.

He got up, got dressed, and went downstairs, meaning to see the thing in pieces before he even had his morning's coffee.

CHAPTER ELEVEN

Kevin wished his *first* visit to the two-dimensional town of Polaroidsville had also been his *last* visit there, but that was not the case. During the thirteen nights since the first one, he'd had the dream more and more often. If the dumb dream happened to take the night off—*little vacation, Kev, but seeya soon, okay?*—he was apt to have it twice the next night. Now he always *knew* it was a dream, and as soon as it started he would tell himself that all he had to do was wake himself up, *dammit, just wake yourself up!* Sometimes he *did* wake up, and sometimes the dream just faded back into deeper sleep, but he never succeeded in waking *himself* up.

It was always Polaroidsville now—never Oatley or Hildasville, those first two efforts of his fumbling mind to identify the place. And like the photograph, each dream took the action just a little bit further. First the man with the shopping-cart, which was never empty now even to start with but filled with a jumble of objects . . . mostly clocks, but all from the Emporium Galorium, and all with the eerie look not of real things but rather of *photographs* of real things which had been cut out of magazines and then somehow, impossibly, paradoxically, stuffed into a shopping-cart, which, since it was as two-dimensional as the objects themselves, had no breadth in which to store them. Yet there they were, and the old man hunched protectively over them and told Kevin to get out, that he was a fushing feef . . . only now he also told Kevin that if he *didn't* get out, "I'll sic Pop's dawg on you! Fee if I don't!"

The fat woman who couldn't be fat since she was perfectly flat but who was fat anyway came next. She appeared pushing her own shopping-cart filled with Polaroid Sun cameras. She also spoke to him before he passed her. "Be careful, boy," she'd say in the loud but toneless voice of one who is utterly deaf, "Pop's dog broke his leash and he's a mean un. He tore up three or four people at the Trenton Farm in Camberville before he came here. It's hard to take his pitcher, but you can't do it at all, 'less you have a cam'ra."

She would bend to get one, would sometimes get as far as holding it out, and he would reach for the camera, not knowing why the woman would think he should take the dog's picture or why he'd want to . . . or maybe he was just trying to be polite?

Either way, it made no difference. They both moved with the stately slowness of underwater swimmers, as dream-people so often do, and they always just missed making connections; when Kevin thought of this part of the dream, he often thought of the famous picture of God and Adam which Michelangelo had painted on the ceiling of the Sistine Chapel: each of them with an arm outstretched, and each with the hand at the end of the arm also outstretched, and the forefingers almost—not quite, but *almost*—touching.

Then she would disappear for a moment because she had no width, and when she reappeared again she was out of reach. *Well just go back to her, then,* Kevin would think each time the dream reached this point, but he couldn't. His feet carried him heedlessly and serenely onward to the peeling white picket fence and Pop and the dog . . . only the dog was no longer a dog but some horrible mixed thing that gave off heat and smoke like a dragon and had the teeth and twisted, scarred snout of a wild pig. Pop and the Sun dog would turn toward him at the same time, and Pop would have the camera—*his* camera, Kevin knew, because there was a piece chipped out of the side—up to his right eye. His left eye was squinted shut. His rimless spectacles glinted on top of his head in hazy sunlight. Pop and the Sun dog had all three dimensions. They were the only things in this seedy, creepy little dreamtown that did.

"He's the one!" Pop cried in a shrill, fearful voice. "He's the thief! Sic em, boy! *Pull his fuckin guts out, is what I mean to say!*"

And as he screamed out this last, heatless lightning flashed in the day as Pop triggered the shutter and the flash, and Kevin turned to run. The dream had stopped here the second time he had had it. Now, on each subsequent occasion, things went a little further. Again he was moving with the aquatic slowness of a performer in an underwater ballet. He felt that, if he had been outside himself, he would even have *looked* like a dancer, his arms turning like the blades of a propeller just starting up, his shirt twisting with his body, pulling taut across his chest and his belly at the same time he heard the shirt's tail pulling free of his pants at the small of his back with a magnified rasp like sandpaper.

Then he was running back the way he came, each foot rising slowly and then floating dreamily (of *course* dreamily, what else, you fool? he would think at this point every time) back down until it hit the cracked and listless cement of the sidewalk, the soles of his tennis shoes flattening as they took his weight and spanking up small clouds of grit moving so slowly that he could see the individual particles revolving like atoms.

He ran slowly, yes, of course, and the Sun dog, nameless stray Grendel of a thing that came from nowhere and signified nothing and had all the sense of a cyclone but existed nevertheless, chased him slowly . . . but not *quite* as slowly.

On the third night, the dream faded into normal sleep just as Kevin began to turn his head in that dragging, maddening slow motion to see how much of a lead he had on the dog. It then skipped a night. On the following night it returned— twice. In the first dream he got his head halfway around so he could see the street on his left disappearing into limbo behind him as he ran along it; in the second (and from this one his alarm-clock woke him, sweating lightly in a crouched fetal position on the far side of the bed) he got his head turned enough to see the dog just as its forepaws came down in his own tracks, and he saw the paws were digging crumbly little craters in the cement because they had sprouted claws . . . and from the back of each lower leg-joint there protruded a long thorn of bone that looked like a spur. The thing's muddy reddish eye was locked on Kevin. Dim fire blew and dripped from its nostrils. *Jesus, Jesus Christ, its SNOT'S on fire,* Kevin thought, and when he woke he was horrified to hear himself whispering it over and over, very rapidly: ". . . snot's on fire, snot's on fire, snot's on fire."

Night by night the dog gained on him as he fled down the sidewalk. Even when he wasn't turning to look he could *hear* the Sun dog gaining. He was aware of a spread of warmth from his crotch and knew he was in enough fear to have wet himself, although the emotion came through in the same diluted, numbed way he seemed to have to move in this world. He could hear the Sun dog's paws striking the cement, could hear the dry crack and squall of the cement breaking. He could hear the hot blurts of its breath, the suck of air flowing in past those outrageous teeth.

And on the night Pop woke up to find he had not only walked in his sleep but taken at least one picture in it, Kevin *felt* as well as heard the Sun dog's breath for the first time: a warm rush of air on his buttocks like the sultry suck of wind a subway on an express run pulls through a station where it needn't stop. He knew the dog was close enough to spring on his back now, and that would come next; he would feel one more breath, this one not just warm but *hot,* as hot as acute indigestion in your throat, and then that crooked living bear-trap of a mouth would sink deep into the flesh of his back, between the shoulderblades, ripping the skin and meat off his spine, and did he think this was really just a dream? *Did* he?

He awoke from this last one just as Pop was gaining the top of the stairs to his apartment and resting one final time before going inside back to bed. This time Kevin woke sitting bolt upright, the sheet and blanket which had been over him puddled around his waist, his skin covered with sweat and yet *freezing,* a million stiff little white goose-pimples standing out all over his belly, chest, back, and arms like stigmata. Even his cheeks seemed to crawl with them.

And what he thought about was not the dream, or at least not directly; he thought instead: *It's wrong, the number is wrong, it says three but it can't—*

Then he flopped back and, in the way of children (for even at fifteen most of him was still a child and would be until later that day), he fell into a deep sleep again.

The alarm woke him at seven-thirty, as it always did on school mornings, and he found himself sitting up in bed again, wide-eyed, every piece suddenly in place. The Sun he had smashed hadn't been *his* Sun, and that was why he kept having this same crazy dream over and over and over again. Pop Merrill, that kindly old crackerbarrel philosopher and repairer of cameras and clocks and small appliances, had euchred him and his father as neatly and competently as a riverboat gambler does the tenderfeet in an old Western movie.

His father—!

He heard the door downstairs slam shut and leaped out of bed. He took two running strides toward the door in his underwear, thought better of it, turned, yanked the window up, and hollered *"Dad!"* just as his father was folding himself into the car to go to work.

CHAPTER TWELVE

Pop dredged his key-ring up from his pocket, unlocked the "special" drawer, and took out the camera, once again being careful to hold it by the strap only. He looked with some hope at the front of the Polaroid, thinking he might see that the lens had been smashed in its latest tumble, hoping that the goddam thing's eye had been poked out, you might say, but his father had been fond of saying that the devil's luck is always in, and that seemed to be the case with Kevin Delevan's goddamned camera. The chipped place on the thing's side had chipped away a little more, but that was all.

He closed the drawer and, as he turned the key, saw the one picture he'd taken in his sleep lying face-down on the floor. As unable not to look at it as Lot's wife had been unable not to turn back and look at the destruction of Sodom, he picked it up with those blunt fingers that hid their dexterity from the world so well and turned it over.

The dog-creature had begun its spring. Its forepaws had barely left the ground, but along its misshapen backbone and in the bunches of muscle under the hide with its hair like the stiff filaments sticking out of black steel brushes he could see all that kinetic energy beginning to release itself. Its face and head were actually a little blurred in this photograph as its mouth yawned wider, and drifting up from the picture, like a sound heard under glass, he seemed to hear a low and throaty snarl beginning to rise toward a roar. The shadow-photographer looked as if he were trying to stumble back another pace, but what did it matter? That was smoke jetting from the holes in the dog-thing's muzzle, all right, *smoke,* and

134

more smoke drifting back from the hinges of its open jaws in the little space where the croggled and ugly stake-wall of its teeth ended, and any man would stumble back from a horror like *that,* any man would try to turn and run, but all Pop had to do was look to tell you that the man (of *course* it was a man, maybe once it had been a boy, a teenage boy, but who had the camera now?) who had taken that picture in mere startled reflex, with a kind of wince of the finger . . . that man didn't have a nickel's worth of chances. That man could keep his feet or trip over them, and all the difference it would make would be as to how he died: while he was on his feet or while he was on his ass.

Pop crumpled the picture between his fingers and then stuck his key-ring back into his pocket. He turned, holding what had been Kevin Delevan's Polaroid Sun 660 and was now *his* Polaroid Sun 660 by the strap and started toward the back of the store; he would pause on the way just long enough to get the sledge. And as he neared the door to the back shed, a shutterflash, huge and white and soundless, went off not in front of his eyes but behind them, in his brain.

He turned back, and now his eyes were as empty as the eyes of a man who has been temporarily blinded by some bright light. He walked past the worktable with the camera now held in his hands at chest level, as one might carry a votive urn or some other sort of religious offering or relic. Halfway between the worktable and the front of the store was a bureau covered with clocks. To its left was one of the barnlike structure's support beams, and from a hook planted in this there hung another clock, an imitation German cuckoo clock. Pop grasped it by the roof and pulled it off its hook, indifferent to the counterweights, which immediately became entangled in one another's chains, and to the pendulum, which snapped off when one of the disturbed chains tried to twine around it. The little door below the roofpeak of the clock sprang ajar; the wooden bird poked out its beak and one startled eye. It gave a single choked sound—*kook!*—as if in protest of this rough treatment before creeping back inside again.

Pop hung the Sun by its strap on the hook where the clock had been, then turned and moved toward the back of the store for the second time, his eyes still blank and dazzled. He clutched the clock by its roof, swinging it back and forth indifferently, not hearing the cluds and clunks from inside it, or the occasional strangled sound that might have been the bird trying to escape, not noticing when one of the counter-weights smacked the end of an old bed, snapped off, and went rolling beneath, leaving a deep trail in the undisturbed dust of years. He moved with the blank mindless purpose of a robot. In the shed, he paused just long enough to pick up the sledge-hammer by its smooth shaft. With both hands thus filled, he had to use the elbow of his left arm to knock the hook out of the eyebolt so he could push open the shed door and walk into the backyard.

He crossed to the chopping block and set the imitation German cuckoo clock on it. He stood for a moment with his head inclined down toward it, both of his hands now on the handle of the sledge. His face remained blank, his eyes dim and dazzled, but there was a part of his mind which not only thought clearly but thought *all* of him was thinking—and acting—clearly. This part of him saw not a cuckoo clock which hadn't been worth much to begin with and was now broken in the bargain; it saw Kevin's Polaroid. This part of his mind really believed he had come downstairs, gotten the Polaroid from the drawer, and proceeded directly out back, pausing only to get the sledge.

And it was this part that would do his remembering later . . . unless it became convenient for him to remember some other truth. Or any other truth, for that matter.

Pop Merrill raised the sledgehammer over his right shoulder and brought it down hard—not as hard as Kevin had done, but hard enough to do the job. It struck squarely on the roof of the imitation German cuckoo clock. The clock did not so much break or shatter as *splatter;* pieces of plastic wood and little gears and springs flew everywhere. And what that little piece of Pop which saw would remember (unless, of course, it became convenient to remember otherwise) were pieces of *camera* splattering everywhere.

He pulled the sledge off the block and stood for a moment with his meditating, unseeing eyes on the shambles. The bird, which to Pop looked exactly like a film-case, a Polaroid Sun film-case, was lying on its back with its little wooden feet sticking straight up in the air, looking both deader than any bird outside of a cartoon ever looked and yet somehow miraculously unhurt at the same time. He had his look, then turned and headed back toward the shed door.

"There," he muttered under his breath. "Good 'nuff."

Someone standing even very close to him might have been unable to pick up the words themselves, but it would have been hard to miss the unmistakable tone of relief with which they were spoken.

"*That's* done. Don't have to worry about *that* anymore. Now what's next? Pipe-tobacco, isn't it?"

But when he got to the drugstore on the other side of the block fifteen minutes later, it was not pipe-tobacco he asked for (although that was what he would *remember* asking for). He asked for film.

Polaroid film.

CHAPTER THIRTEEN

"Kevin, I'm going to be late for work if I don't—"

"Will you call in? Can you? Call in and say you'll be late, or that you might not get there at all? If it was something really, really, *really* important?"

Warily, Mr. Delevan asked, "What's the something?"

"*Could* you?"

Mrs. Delevan was standing in the doorway of Kevin's bedroom now. Meg was behind her. Both of them were eyeing the man in his business suit and the tall boy, still wearing only his Jockey shorts, curiously.

"I suppose I—yes, say I could. But I won't until I know what it *is.*"

Kevin lowered his voice, and, cutting his eyes toward the door, he said: "It's about Pop Merrill. And the camera."

Mr. Delevan, who had at first only looked puzzled at what Kevin's eyes were doing, now went to the door. He murmured something to his wife, who nodded. Then he closed the door, paying no more attention to Meg's protesting whine than he would have to a bird singing a bundle of notes on a telephone wire outside the bedroom window.

"What did you tell Mom?" Kevin asked.

"That it was man-to-man stuff." Mr. Delevan smiled a little. "I think *she* thinks you want to talk about masturbating."

Kevin flushed.

Mr. Delevan looked concerned. "You don't, do you? I mean, you know about—"

"I know, I know," Kevin said hastily; he was not about to tell his father (and wasn't sure he would have been able to put the

138

right string of words together, even if he had wanted to) that what had thrown him momentarily off-track was finding out that not only did his *father* know about whacking off—which of course shouldn't have surprised him at all but somehow did, leaving him with feelings of surprise at his own surprise—but that his *mother* somehow did, too.

Never mind. All this had nothing to do with the nightmares, or with the new certainty which had locked into place in his head.

"It's about Pop, I told you. And some bad dreams I've been having. But mostly it's about the camera. Because Pop stole it somehow, Dad."

"Kevin—"

"I beat it to pieces on his chopping block, I know. But it wasn't *my* camera. It was *another* camera. And that isn't even the worst thing. The worst thing is that *he's still using mine to take pictures!* And that dog is going to get out! When it does, I think it's going to kill me. In that other world it's already started to j-j-j—"

He couldn't finish. Kevin surprised himself again—this time by bursting into tears.

By the time John Delevan got his son calmed down it was ten minutes of eight, and he had resigned himself to at least being late for work. He held the boy in his arms—whatever it was, it really had the kid shook, and if it really *was* nothing but a bunch of dreams, Mr. Delevan supposed he would find sex at the root of the matter someplace.

When Kevin was shivering and only sucking breath deep into his lungs in an occasional dry-sob, Mr. Delevan went to the door and opened it cautiously, hoping Mary had taken Meg downstairs. She had; the hallway was empty. *That's one for our side, anyway,* he thought, and went back to Kevin.

"Can you talk now?" he asked.

"Pop's got my camera," Kevin said hoarsely. His red eyes,

still watery, peered at his father almost myopically. "He got it somehow, and he's using it."

"And this is something you *dreamed?*"

"Yes . . . and I remembered something."

"Kevin . . . that *was* your camera. I'm sorry, son, but it *was.* I even saw the little chip in the side."

"He must have rigged that somehow—"

"Kevin, that seems pretty farf—"

"Listen," Kevin said urgently, "will you just *listen?*"

"All right. Yes. I'm listening."

"What I remembered was that when he handed me the camera—when we went out back to crunch it, remember?"

"Yes—"

"I looked in the little window where the camera keeps count of how many shots there are left. And it said three, Dad! It said *three!*"

"Well? What about it?"

"It had film in it, too! *Film!* I know, because I remember one of those shiny black things jumping up when I squashed the camera. It jumped up and then it fluttered back down."

"I repeat: so what?"

"There wasn't any film in my camera when I gave it to Pop! That's so-what. I had twenty-eight pictures. He wanted me to take thirty more, for a total of fifty-eight. I might have bought more film if I'd known what he was up to, but probably not. By then I was scared of the thing—"

"Yeah. I was, a little, too."

Kevin looked at him respectfully. "Were you?"

"Yeah. Go on. I think I see where you're heading."

"I was just going to say, he chipped in for the film, but not enough—not even half. He's a *wicked* skinflint, Dad."

John Delevan smiled thinly. "He is that, my boy. One of the world's greatest, is what I mean to say. Go on and finish up. *Tempus* is *fugiting* away like mad."

Kevin glanced at the clock. It was almost eight. Although

neither of them knew it, Pop would wake up in just under two minutes and start about his morning's business, very little of which he would remember correctly.

"All right," Kevin said. "All I'm trying to say is I couldn't have bought any more film even if I'd wanted to. I used up all the money I had buying the three film packs. I even borrowed a buck from Megan, so I let her shoot a couple, too."

"Between the two of you, you used up *all* the exposures? Every single one?"

"Yes! *Yes!* He even *said* it was fifty-eight! And between the time when I finished shooting all the pictures he wanted and when we went to look at the tape he made, I never bought any more film. It was *dead empty* when I brought it in, Dad! The number in the little window was a *zero!* I saw it, I remember! So if it was my camera, how come it said *three* in the window when we went back downstairs?"

"He *couldn't* have—" Then his father stopped, and a queer look of uncharacteristic gloom came over his face as he realized that Pop *could* have, and that the truth of it was this: he, John Delevan, didn't want to believe that Pop *had;* that even bitter experience had not been sufficient vaccination against foolishness, and Pop might have pulled the wool over his own eyes as well as those of his son.

"Couldn't have *what?* What are you thinking about, Dad? Something just hit you!"

Something had hit him, all right. How eager Pop had been to go downstairs and get the original Polaroids so they could all get a closer look at the thing around the dog's neck, the thing that turned out to be Kevin's latest string tie from Aunt Hilda, the one with the bird on it that was probably a woodpecker.

We might as well go down with you, Kevin had said when Pop had offered to get the photos, but hadn't Pop jumped up himself, chipper as a chickadee? *Won't take a minute,* the old man had said, or some such thing, and the truth was, Mr. Delevan told himself, I hardly noticed *what* he was saying or doing,

141

because I wanted to watch that goddamned tape again. And the truth *also* was this: Pop hadn't even had to pull the old switcheroo right in front of them—although, with his eyes unwooled, Mr. Delevan was reluctantly willing to believe the old son of a bitch had probably been prepared to do just that, if he had to, and probably *could* have done it, too, pushing seventy or not. With them upstairs and him downstairs, presumably doing no more than getting Kevin's photographs, he could have swapped *twenty* cameras, at his leisure.

"Dad?"

"I suppose he could have," Mr. Delevan said. "But why?"

Kevin could only shake his head. He didn't know why. But that was all right; Mr. Delevan thought *he* did, and it was something of a relief. Maybe honest men *didn't* have to learn the world's simplest truths over and over again; maybe some of those truths eventually stuck fast. He'd only had to articulate the question aloud in order to find the answer. Why did the Pop Merrills of this world do anything? To make a profit. That was the reason, the whole reason, and nothing but the reason. Kevin had wanted to destroy it. After looking at Pop's videotape, Mr. Delevan had found himself in accord with that. Of the three of them, who had been the only one capable of taking a longer view?

Why, Pop, of course. Reginald Marion "Pop" Merrill.

John Delevan had been sitting on the edge of Kevin's bed with an arm about his son's shoulders. Now he stood up. "Get dressed. I'll go downstairs and call in. I'll tell Brandon I'll probably just be late, but to assume I won't be in at all."

He was preoccupied with this, already talking to Brandon Reed in his mind, but not so preoccupied he didn't see the gratitude which lighted his son's worried face. Mr. Delevan smiled a little and felt that uncharacteristic gloom first ease and then let go entirely. There was this much, at least: his son was as yet not too old to take comfort from him, or accept him as a higher power to whom appeals could sometimes be directed in the knowledge that they would be acted upon; nor was he himself too old to take comfort from his son's comfort.

"I think," he said, moving toward the door, "that we ought to pay a call on Pop Merrill." He glanced at the clock on Kevin's night-table. It was ten minutes after eight, and in back of the Emporium Galorium, a sledgehammer was coming down on an imitation German cuckoo clock. "He usually opens around eight-thirty. Just about the time we'll get there, I think. If you get a wiggle on, that is."

He paused on his way out and a brief, cold smile flickered on his mouth. He was not smiling at his son. "I think he's got some explaining to do, is what I mean to say."

Mr. Delevan went out, closing the door behind him. Kevin quickly began to dress.

CHAPTER FOURTEEN

The Castle Rock LaVerdiere's Super Drug Store was a lot more than just a drugstore. Put another way, it was really only a drugstore as an afterthought. It was as if someone had noticed at the last moment—just before the grand opening, say—that one of the words in the sign was still "Drug." That someone might have made a mental note to tell someone else, someone in the company's management, that here they were, opening yet another LaVerdiere's, and they had by simple oversight neglected yet again to correct the sign so it read, more simply and accurately, LaVerdiere's Super Store . . . and, after making the mental note, the someone in charge of noticing such things had delayed the grand opening a day or two so they could shoe-horn in a prescription counter about the size of a telephone booth in the long building's furthest, darkest, and most neglected corner.

The LaVerdiere's Super Drug Store was really more of a jumped-up five-and-dime than anything else. The town's last *real* five-and-dime, a long dim room with feeble, fly-specked overhead globes hung on chains and reflected murkily in the creaking but often-waxed wooden floor, had been The Ben Franklin Store. It had given up the ghost in 1978 to make way for a video-games arcade called Galaxia and E-Z Video Rentals, where Tuesday was Toofers Day and no one under the age of twenty could go in the back room.

LaVerdiere's carried everything the old Ben Franklin had carried, but the goods were bathed in the pitiless light of Maxi-Glo fluorescent bars which gave every bit of stock its own hectic, feverish shimmer. *Buy me!* each item seemed to shriek. *Buy me or you may die! Or your wife may die! Or your kids! Or your best friend! Possibly all of them at once! Why? How should I know? I'm just a brainless item sitting on a pre-fab LaVerdiere's shelf! But doesn't it feel true? You know it does! So buy me and buy me* RIGHT . . . NOW!

There was an aisle of notions, two aisles of first-aid supplies and nostrums, an aisle of video and audio tapes (both blank and pre-recorded). There was a long rack of magazines giving way to paperback books, a display of lighters under one digital cash-register and a display of watches under another (a third register was hidden in the dark corner where the pharmacist lurked in his lonely shadows). Halloween candy had taken over most of the toy aisle (the toys would not only come back after Halloween but eventually take over two whole aisles as the days slid remorselessly down toward Christmas). And, like something too neat to exist in reality except as a kind of dumb admission that there *was* such a thing as Fate with a capital F, and that Fate might, in its own way, indicate the existence of that whole "other world" about which Pop had never before cared (except in terms of how it might fatten his pocketbook, that was) and about which Kevin Delevan had never before even thought, at the front of the store, in the main display area, was a carefully arranged work of salesmanship which was billed as the FALL FOTO FESTIVAL.

This display consisted of a basket of colorful autumn leaves spilling out on the floor in a bright flood (a flood too large to actually have come from that one basket alone, a careful observer might have concluded). Amid the leaves were a number of Kodak and Polaroid cameras—several Sun 660s among the latter—and all sorts of other equipment: cases, albums, film, flashbars. In the midst of this odd cornucopia, an old-fashioned tripod rose like one of H. G. Wells's Martian death-machines towering over the crispy wreck of London. It bore a sign which told all patrons interested enough to look that this week one could obtain SUPER REDUCTIONS ON ALL POLAROID CAMERAS & ACCESSORIES!

145

At eight-thirty that morning, half an hour after LaVerdiere's opened for the day, "all patrons" consisted of Pop Merrill and Pop alone. He took no notice of the display but marched straight to the only open counter, where Molly Durham had just finished laying out the watches on their imitation-velvet display-cloth.

Oh no, here comes old Eyeballs, she thought, and grimaced. Pop's idea of a really keen way to kill a stretch of time about as long as Molly's coffee-break was to kind of *ooze* up to the counter where she was working (he always picked hers, even if he had to stand in line; in fact, she thought he liked it better when there *was* a line) and buy a pouch of Prince Albert tobacco. This was a purchase an ordinary fellow could transact in maybe thirty seconds, but if she got Eyeballs out of her face in under three minutes, she thought she was doing very well indeed. He kept all of his money in a cracked leather purse on a chain, and he'd haul it out of his pocket—giving his doorbells a good feel on the way, it always looked to Molly—and then open it. It always gave out a little *screeeeek!* noise, and honest to God if you didn't expect to see a moth flutter out of it, just like in those cartoons people draw of tightwads. On top of the purse's contents there would be a whole mess of paper money, bills that looked somehow as if you shouldn't handle them, as if they might be coated with disease germs of some kind, and jingling silver underneath. Pop would fish out a dollar bill and then kind of hook the other bills to one side with one of those thick fingers of his to get to the change underneath—he'd never give you a couple of bucks, hunh-uh, that would make everything too quick to suit him—and then he'd work *that* out, too. And all the time his eyes would be busy, flicking down to the purse for a second or two but mostly letting the fingers sort out the proper coins by touch while his eyes crawled over her boobs, her belly, her hips, and then back up to her boobs again. Never once her face; not even so far as her mouth, which *was* a part of a girl in which most men seemed to be interested; no, Pop Merrill was strictly interested in the lower portions of the female anatomy. When he finally finished—and no matter how quick that was, it always seemed like three times as long to Molly—and got the hell out of the store again, she always felt like going somewhere and taking a long shower.

So she braced herself, put on her best it's-only-eight-thirty-and-I've-got-seven-and-a-half-hours-to-go smile, and stood at the counter as Pop approached. She told herself, *He's only looking at you, guys have been doing that since you sprouted,* and that was true, but this wasn't the same. Because Pop Merrill wasn't like most of the guys who had run their eyes over her trim and eminently watchable superstructure since that time ten years ago. Part of it was that Pop was *old,* but that wasn't all of it. The truth was that some guys looked at you and some—a very few—seemed to actually be feeling you up with their eyes, and Merrill was one of *those.* His gaze actually seemed to have weight; when he fumbled in his creaky old-maid's purse on its length of incongruously masculine chain, she seemed to actually *feel* his eyes squirming up and down her front, lashing their way up her hills on their optic nerves like tadpoles and then sliding bonelessly down into her valleys, making her wish she had worn a nun's habit to work that day. Or maybe a suit of armor.

But her mother had been fond of saying *What can't be cured must be endured, sweet Molly,* and until someone discovered a method of weighing gazes so those of dirty men both young and old could be outlawed, or, more likely, until Pop Merrill did everyone in Castle Rock a favor by dying so that eyesore of a tourist trap he kept could be torn down, she would just have to deal with it as best she could.

But today she was in for a pleasant surprise—or so it seemed at first. Pop's usual hungry appraisal was not even an ordinary patron's look; it seemed utterly blank. It wasn't that he looked through her, or that his gaze struck her and bounced off. It seemed to Molly that he was so deep in his thoughts that his usually penetrating look did not even reach her, but made it about halfway and then petered out—like a man trying to locate and observe a star on the far side of the galaxy with just the naked eye.

"May I help you, Mr. Merrill?" she asked, and her feet were already cocking so she could turn quickly and reach up for where the pouches of tobacco were kept. With Pop, this was a task she always did as quickly as possible, because when she turned and reached, she could feel his eyes crawling busily over her ass, dropping for a quick check of her legs, then rising again to her butt for a final ocular squeeze and perhaps a pinch before she turned back.

"Yes," he said calmly and serenely, and he might as well have been talking to one of those automated bank machines for all the interest in her he showed. That was fine by Molly. "I'd like some" and then either a word she didn't hear right or one that was utter gibberish. If it was gobbledegook, she thought with some hope, maybe the first few parts of the complicated network of dikes, levees, and spillways the old crock had constructed against the rising sea of senility were finally giving way.

It *sounded* as if he had said *toefilmacco,* which wasn't a product they stocked . . . unless it was a prescription drug of some sort.

"I beg pardon, Mr. Merrill?"

"Film," he said, so clearly and firmly that Molly was more than disappointed; she was convinced he must have said it just that way the first time and her ears had picked it up wrong. Maybe *she* was the one who was beginning to lose her dikes and levees.

"What kind would you like?"

"Polaroid," he said. "Two packs." She didn't know exactly what was going on here, but it was beyond doubt that Castle Rock's premier dirty old man was not himself today. His eyes would still not focus, and the words . . . they reminded her

148

of something, something she associated with her five-year-old niece, Ellen, but she couldn't catch hold of it.

"For what model, Mr. Merrill?"

She sounded brittle and actressy to herself, but Pop Merrill didn't even come close to noticing. Pop was lost in the ozone.

After a moment's consideration in which he did not look at her at all but seemed instead to study the racks of cigarettes behind her left shoulder, he jerked out: "For a Polaroid Sun camera. Model 660." And then it came to her, even as she told him she'd have to get it from the display. Her niece owned a big soft panda toy, which she had, for reasons which would probably make sense only to another little girl, named Paulette. Somewhere inside of Paulette was an electronic circuit-board and a memory chip on which were stored about four hundred short, simple sentences such as "I like to hug, don't you?" and "I wish you'd *never* go away." Whenever you poked Paulette above her fuzzy little navel, there was a brief pause and then one of those lovesome little remarks would come out, almost *jerk* out, in a somehow remote and emotionless voice that seemed by its tone to deny the content of the words. Ellen thought Paulette was the nuts. Molly thought there was something creepy about it; she kept expecting Ellen to poke the panda-doll in the guts someday and it would surprise them all (except for Aunt Molly from Castle Rock) by saying what was *really* on its mind. "I think tonight after you're asleep I'll strangle you dead," perhaps, or maybe just "I have a knife."

Pop Merrill sounded like Paulette the stuffed panda this morning. His blank gaze was uncannily like Paulette's. Molly had thought any change from the old man's usual leer would be a welcome one. She had been wrong.

Molly bent over the display, for once totally unconscious of the way her rump was poking out, and tried to find what the old man wanted as quickly as she could. She was sure that when she turned around, Pop would be looking at anything but her. This time she was right. When she had the film and started back (brushing a couple of errant fall leaves from one of the boxes), Pop was still staring at the cigarette racks, at first glance appearing to look so closely he might have been inventorying the stock. It took a second or two to see that that expression was no expression at all, really, but a gaze of almost divine blankness.

Please get out of here, Molly prayed. *Please, just take your film and go. And whatever else you do, don't touch me. Please.*

If he touched her while he was looking like that, Molly thought she would scream. Why did the place have to be empty? Why couldn't at least one other customer be in here, preferably Sheriff Pangborn, but since he seemed to be otherwise engaged, anyone at all? She supposed Mr. Constantine, the pharmacist, was in the store someplace, but the drug counter looked easily a quarter of a mile away, and while she knew it *couldn't* be that far, not really, it was still too far for him to reach her in a hurry if old man Merrill decided to touch her. And suppose Mr. Constantine had gone out to Nan's for coffee with Mr. Keeton from the selectmen's office? The more she thought about that possibility, the more likely it seemed. When something genuinely weird like this happened, wasn't it an almost foregone conclusion that it should happen while one was alone?

He's having a mental breakdown of some kind.

She heard herself saying with glassy cheerfulness: "Here you are, Mr. Merrill." She put the film on the counter and scooted to her left and behind the register at once, wanting it between her and him.

The ancient leather purse came out of Pop Merrill's pants, and her stuttering fingers miskeyed the purchase so she had to clear the register and start again.

He was holding two ten-dollar bills out to her.

She told herself they were only *rumpled* from being squashed up with the other bills in that little pocketbook, probably not even old, although they *looked* old. That didn't stop her galloping mind, however. Her mind insisted that they weren't just *rumpled,* they were rumpled and *slimy.* It further insisted that *old* wasn't the right word, that *old* wasn't even in the ball-park. For those particular items of currency, not even the word *ancient* would do. Those were *prehistoric* tens, somehow printed before Christ was born and Stonehenge was built, before the first low-browed, no-neck Neanderthal had crawled out of his cave. They belonged to a time when even God had been a baby.

She didn't want to touch them.

She *had* to touch them.

The man would want his change.

Steeling herself, she took the bills and shoved them into the cash register as fast as she could, banging a finger so hard she ripped most of the nail clear off, an ordinarily exquisite pain she would not notice, in her extreme state of distress, until sometime later . . . when, that was, she had chivvied her willing mind around enough to scold herself for acting like a whoopsy little girl on the edge of her first menstrual period.

At the moment, however, she only concentrated on getting the bills into the register as fast as she could and getting her hand *off* them, but even later she would remember what the surfaces of those tens had felt like. It felt as if they were actu-ally crawling and moving under the pads of her fingers; as if billions of germs, *huge* germs almost big enough to be seen with the naked eye, were sliding along them toward her, eager to infect her with whatever *he* had.

But the man would want his change.

She concentrated on that, lips pressed together so tightly they were dead white; four singles that did not, absolutely did *not* want to come out from beneath the roller that held them down in the cash drawer. Then a dime, but oh Jesus-please-us, there *were* no dimes, and what the hell was *wrong* with her, what had she done to be saddled for so long with this weird old man on the one morning in recorded history when he actually seemed to want to get out of here in a hurry?

She fished out a nickel, feeling the silent, stinky loom of him so close to her (and she felt that when she was finally forced to look up she would see he was even closer, that he was leaning over the counter toward her), then three pennies, four, five . . . but the last one dropped back into the drawer among the quarters and she had to fish for it with one of her cold, numb fingers. It almost squirted away from her again; she could feel sweat popping out on the nape of her neck and on the little strip of skin between her nose and her upper lip. Then, clutching the coins tightly in her fist and praying he wouldn't have his hand outstretched to receive them so she would have to touch his dry, reptilian skin, but knowing, somehow *knowing* that he would, she looked up, feeling her bright and cheery LaVerdiere's smile stretching the muscles of her face in a kind of frozen scream, trying to steel herself for even *that,* telling herself it would be the last, and never mind the image her stupid, insisting mind kept trying to make her see, an image of that dry hand suddenly snapping shut over hers like the talon of some old and horrid bird, a bird not of prey, no, not even that, but one of carrion; she told herself she did not see those images, absolutely did *NOT,* and, seeing them all the same, she looked up with that smile screaming off her face as brightly as a cry of murder on a hot still night, and the store was empty.

Pop was gone.

He had left while she was making change.

Molly began to shudder all over. If she had needed concrete proof that the old geezer was not right, this was it. This was proof positive, proof indubitable, proof of the purest ray serene: for the first time in her memory (and in the living memory of the town, she would have bet, and she would have won her bet), Pop Merrill, who refused to tip even on those rare occasions when he was forced to eat in a restaurant that had no take-out service, had left a place of business without waiting for his change.

Molly tried to open her hand and let go of the four ones,

the nickel, and the five pennies. She was stunned to find she couldn't do it. She had to reach over with her other hand and pry the fingers loose. Pop's change dropped to the glass top of the counter and she swept it off to one side, not wanting to touch it.

And she never wanted to see Pop Merrill again.

CHAPTER FIFTEEN

Pop's vacant gaze held as he left LaVerdiere's. It held as he crossed the sidewalk with the boxes of film in his hand. It broke and became an expression of somehow unsettling alertness as he stepped off into the gutter . . . and stopped there, with one foot on the sidewalk and one planted amid the litter of squashed cigarette butts and empty potato-chip bags. Here was another Pop Molly would not have recognized, although there were those who had been sharp-traded by the old man who would have known it quite well. This was neither Merrill the lecher nor Merrill the robot, but Merrill the animal with its wind up. All at once he was *there,* in a way he seldom allowed himself to be *there* in public. Showing so much of one's true self in public was not, in Pop's estimation, a good idea. This morning, however, he was far from being in command of himself, and there was no one out to observe him, anyway. If there had been, that person would not have seen Pop the folksy crackerbarrel philosopher or even Pop the sharp trader, but something like the *spirit* of the man. In that moment of being totally *there,* Pop looked like a rogue dog himself, a stray who has gone feral and now pauses amid a midnight henhouse slaughter, raggedy ears up, head cocked, bloodstreaked teeth showing a little as he hears some sound from the farmer's house and thinks of the shotgun with its wide black holes like a figure eight rolled onto its side. The dog knows nothing of figure eights, but even a dog may recognize the dim shape of eternity if its instincts are honed sharp enough.

Across the town square he could see the urine-yellow front of the Emporium Galorium, standing slightly apart from its nearest neighbors: the vacant building which had housed The Village Wash tub until earlier that year, Nan's Luncheonette, and You Sew and Sew, the dress-and-notions shop run by Evvie Chalmers's great-granddaughter, Polly—a woman of whom we must speak at another time.

There were slant-parking spaces in front of all the shops on Lower Main Street, and all of them were empty . . . except for one, which was just now being filled with a Ford station-wagon Pop recognized. The light throb of its engine was clearly audible in the morning-still air. Then it cut off, the brakelights went out, and Pop pulled back the foot which had been in the gutter and prudently withdrew himself to the corner of LaVerdiere's. Here he stood as still as that dog who has been alerted in the henhouse by some small sound, the sort of sound which might be disregarded in the killing frenzy of dogs neither so old nor so wise as this one.

John Delevan got out from behind the wheel of the station-wagon. The boy got out on the passenger side. They went to the door of the Emporium Galorium. The man began to knock impatiently, loud enough so the sound of it came as clearly to Pop as the sound of the engine had done. Delevan paused, they both listened, and then Delevan started in again, not knocking now but *hammering* at the door, and you didn't have to be a goddam mind-reader to know the man was steamed up.

They know, Pop thought. *Somehow they know. Damned good thing I smashed the fucking camera.*

He stood a moment longer, nothing moving except his hooded eyes, and then he slipped around the corner of the drugstore and into the alley between it and the neighboring bank. He did it so smoothly that a man fifty years younger might have envied the almost effortless agility of the movement.

This morning, Pop figured, it might be a little wiser to go back home by backyard express.

CHAPTER SIXTEEN

When there was still no answer, John Delevan went at the door a third time, hammering so hard he made the glass rattle loosely in its rotting putty gums and hurt his hand. It was hurting his hand that made him realize how angry he was. Not that he felt the anger was in any way unjustified if Merrill had done what Kevin thought he had done—and yes, the more he thought about it, the more John Delevan was sure that Kevin was right. But he was surprised that he hadn't recognized the anger for what it was until just now.

This seems to be a morning for learning about myself, he thought, and there was something schoolmarmish in that. It allowed him to smile and relax a little.

Kevin was not smiling, nor did he look relaxed.

"It seems like one of three things has happened," Mr. Delevan said to his son. "Merrill's either not up, not answering the door, or he figured we were getting warm and he's absconded with your camera." He paused, then actually laughed. "I guess there's a fourth, too. Maybe he died in his sleep."

"He didn't die." Kevin now stood with his head against the dirty glass of the door he mightily wished he had never gone through in the first place. He had his hands cupped around his eyes to make blinders, because the sun rising over the east side of the town square ran a harsh glare across the glass. "Look."

Mr. Delevan cupped his own hands to the sides of his face and pressed his nose to the glass. They stood there side by side, backs to the square, looking into the dimness of the Emporium Galorium like the world's most dedicated window-shoppers.

156

"Well," he said after a few seconds, "it looks like if he absconded he left his shit behind."

"Yeah—but that's not what I mean. Do you see it?"

"See what?"

"Hanging on that post. The one by the bureau with all the clocks on it."

And after a moment, Mr. Delevan did see it: a Polaroid camera, hanging by its strap from a hook on the post. He thought he could even see the chipped place, although that might have been his imagination.

It's not your imagination.

The smile faded off his lips as he realized he was starting to feel what Kevin was feeling: the weird and distressing certainty that some simple yet terribly dangerous piece of machinery was running . . . and unlike most of Pop's clocks, it was running right on time.

"Do you think he's just sitting upstairs and waiting for us to go away?" Mr. Delevan spoke aloud, but he was really talking to himself. The lock on the door looked both new and expensive . . . but he was willing to bet that if one of them—probably Kevin was in better shape—hit the door hard enough, it would rip right through the old wood. He mused randomly: *A lock is only as good as the door you put it in. People never think.*

Kevin turned his strained face to look at his father. In that moment, John Delevan was as struck by Kevin's face as Kevin had been by his not long ago. He thought: *I wonder how many fathers get a chance to see what their sons will look like as men? He won't always look this strained, this tightly drawn—God, I hope not—but this is what he will look like. And, Jesus, he's going to be handsome!*

He, like Kevin, had that one moment in the midst of whatever it was that was going on here, and the moment was a short one, but he also never forgot; it was always within his mind's reach.

"What?" Kevin asked hoarsely. "What, Dad?"

"You want to bust it? Because I'd go along."

"Not yet. I don't think we'll have to. I don't think he's here . . . but he's close."

You can't know any such thing. Can't even think it.

But his son *did* think it, and he believed Kevin was right. Some sort of link had been formed between Pop and his son. "Some sort" of link? Get serious. He knew perfectly well what the link was. It was that fucking camera hanging on the wall in there, and the longer this went on, the longer he felt that machinery running, its gears grinding and its vicious unthinking cogs turning, the less he liked it.

Break the camera, break the link, he thought, and said: "Are you sure, Kev?"

"Let's go around to the back. Try the door there."

"There's a gate. He'll keep it locked."

"Maybe we can climb over."

"Okay," Mr. Delevan said, and followed his son down the steps of the Emporium Galorium and around to the alley, wondering as he went if he had lost his mind.

But the gate wasn't locked. Somewhere along the line Pop had forgotten to lock it, and although Mr. Delevan hadn't liked the idea of climbing over the fence, or maybe *falling* over the fence, quite likely tearing the hell out of his balls in the process, he somehow liked the open gate even less. All the same, he and Kevin went through it and into Pop's littered backyard, which not even the drifts of fallen October leaves could improve.

Kevin wove his way through the piles of junk Pop had thrown out but not bothered to take to the dump, and Mr. Delevan followed him. They arrived at the chopping block at about the same time Pop was coming out of Mrs. Althea Linden's backyard and onto Mulberry Street, a block west. He would follow Mulberry Street until he reached the offices of the Wolf Jaw Lumber Company. Although the company's pulp trucks would already be coursing the roads of western Maine and the yowl and yark of the cutters' chainsaws would have been rising from the area's diminishing stands of hardwood since six-thirty or so, no one would come in to man the office until nine, which was still a good fifteen minutes away. At the rear of the lumber company's tiny backyard was a high board fence. It was gated, and this gate *was* locked, but Pop had the key. He would unlock the gate and step through into his own backyard.

Kevin reached the chopping block. Mr. Delevan caught up, followed his son's gaze, and blinked. He opened his mouth to ask what in the hell *this* was all about, then shut it again. He was starting to have an idea of what in the hell it was all about without any aid from Kevin. It wasn't *right* to have such ideas, wasn't *natural,* and he knew from bitter experience (in which Reginald Marion "Pop" Merrill himself had played a part at one point, as he had told his son not so long ago) that doing things on impulse was a good way to reach the wrong decision and go flying off half-cocked, but it didn't matter. Although he did not think it in such terms, it would be fair to say Mr. Delevan just hoped he could apply for readmittance to the Reasonable tribe when this was over.

At first he thought he was looking at the smashed remains of a Polaroid camera. Of course that was just his mind, trying to find a little rationality in repetition; what lay on and around the chopping block didn't look anything at all like a camera, Polaroid or otherwise. All those gears and flywheels could only belong to a clock. Then he saw the dead cartoon-bird and even knew what kind of clock. He opened his mouth to ask Kevin why in God's name Pop would bring a cuckoo clock out back and then sledgehammer it to death. He thought it over again and decided he didn't have to ask, after all. The answer to that was also beginning to come. He didn't *want* it to come, because it pointed to madness on what seemed to Mr. Delevan a grand scale, but that didn't matter; it came anyway.

You had to hang a cuckoo clock on something. You had to hang it because of the pendulum weights. And what did you hang it on? Why, a hook, of course.

Maybe a hook sticking out of a beam.

Like the beam Kevin's Polaroid had been hanging on.

Now he spoke, and his words seemed to come from some long distance away: "What in the hell is wrong with him, Kevin? Has he gone nuts?"

"Not *gone,*" Kevin answered, and his voice also seemed to come from some long distance away as they stood above the chopping block, looking down on the busted timepiece. "*Driven* there. By the camera."

"We've got to smash it," Mr. Delevan said. His voice seemed to float to his ears long after he had felt the words coming out of his mouth.

"Not yet," Kevin said. "We have to go to the drugstore first. They're having a special sale on them."

"Having a special sale on wh—"

Kevin touched his arm. John Delevan looked at him. Kevin's head was up, and he looked like a deer scenting fire. In that moment the boy was more than handsome; he was almost divine, like a young poet at the hour of his death.

"What?" Mr. Delevan asked urgently.

"Did you hear something?" Alertness slowly changing to doubt.

"A car on the street," Mr. Delevan said. How much older was he than his son? he wondered suddenly. Twenty-five years? Jesus, wasn't it time he started acting it?

He pushed the strangeness away from him, trying to get it at arm's length. He groped desperately for his maturity and found a little of it. Putting it on was like putting on a badly tattered overcoat.

"You sure that's all it was, Dad?"

"Yes. Kevin, you're wound up too tight. Get hold of your-self or . . ." Or what? But he knew, and laughed shakily. "Or you'll have us both running like a pair of rabbits."

Kevin looked at him thoughtfully for a moment, like some-one coming out of a deep sleep, perhaps even a trance, and then nodded. "Come on."

"Kevin, why? What do you want? He could be upstairs, just not answering—"

"I'll tell you when we get there, Dad. Come *on.*" And almost dragged his father out of the littered backyard and into the narrow alleyway.

"Kevin, do you want to take my arm off, or what?" Mr. Del-evan asked when they got back to the sidewalk.

"He was back there," Kevin said. "Hiding. Waiting for us to go. I felt him."

"He was—" Mr. Delevan stopped, then started again. "Well . . . let's say he was. Just for argument, let's say he was. Shouldn't we go back there and collar him?" And, belatedly: "*Where* was he?"

"On the other side of the fence," Kevin said. His eyes seemed to be floating. Mr. Delevan liked this less all the time. "He's already been. He's already got what *he* needs. We'll have to hurry."

Kevin was already starting for the edge of the sidewalk, meaning to cut across the town square to LaVerdiere's. Mr. Delevan reached out and grabbed him like a conductor grab-bing a fellow he's caught trying to sneak aboard a train with-out a ticket. *"Kevin, what are you talking about?"*

And then Kevin actually said it: looked at him and *said* it. "It's coming, Dad. Please. It's my life." He looked at his father, pleading with his pallid face and his fey, floating eyes. "The dog is coming. It won't do any good to just break in and take the camera. It's gone way past that now. Please don't stop me. Please don't wake me up. It's my *life.*"

Mr. Delevan made one last great effort not to give in to this creeping craziness . . . and then succumbed.

"Come on," he said, hooking his hand around his son's elbow and almost dragging him into the square. "Whatever it is, let's get it done." He paused. "Do we have enough time?"

"I'm not sure," Kevin said, and then, reluctantly: "I don't think so."

CHAPTER SEVENTEEN

Pop waited behind the board fence, looking at the Delevans through a knothole. He had put his tobacco in his back pocket so that his hands would be free to clench and unclench, clench and unclench.

You're on my property, his mind whispered at them, and if his mind had had the power to kill, he would have reached out with it and struck them both dead. *You're on my property, goddammit, you're on my property!*

What he ought to do was go get old John Law and bring him down on their fancy Castle View heads. That was what he *ought* to do. And he would have done it, too, right then, if they hadn't been standing over the wreckage of the camera the boy himself had supposedly destroyed with Pop's blessing two weeks ago. He thought maybe he would have tried to bullshit his way through anyway, but he knew how they felt about him in this town. Pangborn, Keeton, all the rest of them. Trash. That's what they thought of him. Trash.

Until they got their asses in a crack and needed a fast loan and the sun was down, that was.

Clench, unclench. Clench, unclench.

They were talking, but Pop didn't bother listening to what they were saying. His mind was a fuming forge. Now the litany had become: *They're on my goddam property and I can't do a thing about it! They're on my goddam property and I can't do a thing about it! Goddam them! Goddam them!*

At last they left. When he heard the rusty screech of the gate in the alley, Pop used his key on the one in the board fence. He slipped through and ran across the yard to his back

163

door—ran with an unsettling fleetness for a man of seventy, with one hand clapped firmly against his upper right leg, as if, fleet or not, he was fighting a bad rheumatism pain there. In fact, Pop was feeling no pain at all. He didn't want either his keys or the change in his purse jingling, that was all. In case the Delevans were still there, lurking just beyond where he could see. Pop wouldn't have been surprised if they were doing just that. When you were dealing with skunks, you expected them to get up to stinking didos.

He slipped his keys out of his pocket. *Now* they rattled, and although the sound was muted, it seemed very loud to him. He cut his eyes to the left for a moment, sure he would see the brat's staring sheep's face. Pop's mouth was set in a hard, strained grin of fear. There was no one there.

Yet, anyway.

He found the right key, slipped it into the lock, and went in. He was careful not to open the door to the shed too wide, because the hinges picked up a squeal when you exercised them too much.

Inside, he turned the thumb-bolt with a savage twist and then went into the Emporium Galorium. He was more than at home in these shadows. He could have negotiated the narrow, junk-lined corridors in his sleep . . . *had,* in fact, although that, like a good many other things, had slipped his mind for the time being.

There was a dirty little side window near the front of the store that looked out upon the narrow alleyway the Delevans had used to trespass their way into his backyard. It also gave a sharply angled view on the sidewalk and part of the town common.

Pop slipped up to this window between piles of useless, valueless magazines that breathed their dusty yellow museum scent into the dark air. He looked out into the alley and saw it was empty. He looked to the right and saw the Delevans, wavery as fish in an aquarium through this dirty, flawed glass, crossing the common just below the bandstand. He didn't watch them out of sight in this window or go to the front windows to get a better angle on them. He guessed they were going over to LaVerdiere's, and since they had already been here, they would be asking about him. What could the little counter-slut tell them? That he had been and gone. Anything else?

Only that he had bought two pouches of tobacco.

Pop smiled.

That wasn't likely to hang him.

He found a brown bag, went out back, started for the chopping block, considered, then went to the gate in the alleyway instead. Careless once didn't mean a body had to be careless again.

After the gate was locked, he took his bag to the chopping block and picked up the pieces of shattered Polaroid camera. He worked as fast as he could, but he took time to be thorough.

He picked up everything but little shards and splinters that could be seen as no more than anonymous litter. A Police Lab investigating unit would probably be able to ID some of the stuff left around; Pop had seen TV crime shows (when he wasn't watching X-rated movies on his VCR, that was) where those scientific fellows went over the scene of a crime with little brushes and vacuums and even pairs of tweezers, putting things in little plastic bags, but the Castle Rock Sheriff's Department didn't have one of those units. And Pop doubted if Sheriff Pangborn could talk the State Police into sending their crime wagon, even if Pangborn himself could be persuaded to make the effort—not for what was no more than a case of camera theft, and that was all the Delevans could accuse him of without sounding crazy. Once he had policed the area, he went back inside, unlocked his "special" drawer, and deposited the brown bag inside. He relocked the drawer and put his keys back in his pocket. *That* was all right, then. He knew all about search warrants, too. It would be a snowy day in hell before the

Delevans could get Pangborn into district court to ask for one of those. Even if he was crazy enough to try, the remains of the goddamned camera would be gone—*permanently*—long before they could turn the trick. To try and dispose of the pieces for good right now would be more dangerous than leaving them in the locked drawer. The Delevans would come back and catch him right in the middle of it. Best to wait.

Because they *would* be back.

Pop Merrill knew that as well as he knew his own name.

Later, perhaps, after all this hooraw and foolishment died down, he would be able to go to the boy and say *Yes. That's right. Everything you think I did, I did. Now why don't we just leave her alone and go back to not knowin each other . . . all right? We can afford to do that. You might not think so, at least not at first, but we can. Because look—you wanted to bust it up because you thought it was dangerous, and I wanted to sell it because I thought it was valuable. Turned out you was right and I was wrong, and that's all the revenge you're ever gonna need. If you knew me better, you'd know why—there ain't many men in this town that have ever heard me say such a thing. It sticks in my gut, is what I mean to say, but that don't matter; when I'm wrong, I like to think I'm big enough to own up to it, no matter how bad it hurts. In the end, boy, I did what you meant to do in the first place. We all came out on the same street, is what I mean to say, and I think we ought to let bygones be bygones. I know what you think of me, and I know what I think of you, and neither of us would ever vote for the other one to be Grand Marshal in the annual Fourth of July parade, but that's all right; we can live with that, can't we? What I mean to say is just this: we're both glad that goddam camera is gone, so let's call it quits and walk away.*

But that was for later, and even then it was only perhaps. It wouldn't do for right now, that was for sure. They would need time to cool down. Right now both of them would be raring to tear a chunk out of his ass, like

(the dog in that pitcher)

like . . . well, never mind what they'd be like. The impor-

tant thing was to be down here, business as usual and as innocent as a goddam baby when they got back.

Because they *would* be back.

But that was all right. It was all right because—

"B'cause things are under control," Pop whispered. *"That's
what I mean to say."*

Now he did go to the front door, and switched the CLOSED
sign over to OPEN (he then turned it promptly back to CLOSED
again, but this Pop did not observe himself doing, nor would
he remember it later). All right; that was a start. What was
next? Make it look like just another normal day, no more and
no less. He had to be all surprise and what-in-the-tar-nation-
are-you-talking-about when they came back with steam coming out of their collars, all ready to do or die for what had
already been killed just as dead as sheepdip.

So . . . what was the most normal thing they could find him
doing when they came back, with Sheriff Pangborn or without him?

Pop's eye fixed on the cuckoo clock hanging from the beam
beside that nice bureau he'd gotten at an estate sale in Sebago
a month or six weeks ago. Not a very nice cuckoo clock, probably one originally purchased with trading stamps by some soul
trying to be thrifty (people who could only *try* to be thrifty
were, in Pop's estimation, poor puzzled souls who drifted
through life in a vague and constant state of disappointment).
Still, if he could put it right so it would run a little, he could
maybe sell it to one of the skiers who would be up in another
month or two, somebody who needed a clock at their cottage
or ski-lodge because the last bargain had up and died and who
didn't understand yet (and probably never would) that another
bargain wasn't the solution but the problem.

Pop would feel sorry for that person, and would dicker with
him or her as fairly as he thought he could, but he wouldn't
disappoint the buyer. *Caveet emperor* was not only what he *meant*
to say but often *did* say, and he had a living to make, didn't he?

167

Yes. So he would just sit back there at his worktable and fuss around with that clock, see if he could get it running, and when the Delevans got back, that was what they would find him doing. Maybe there'd even be a few prospective customers browsing around by then; he could hope, although this was always a slack time of year. Customers would be icing on the cake, anyway. The important thing was how it would look: just a fellow with nothing to hide, going through the ordinary motions and ordinary rhythms of his ordinary day.

Pop went over to the beam and took the cuckoo clock down, being careful not to tangle up the counterweights. He carried it back to his worktable, humming a little. He set it down, then felt his back pocket. Fresh tobacco. That was good, too.

Pop thought he would have himself a little pipe while he worked.

CHAPTER EIGHTEEN

"You can't *know* he was in here, Kevin!" Mr. Delevan was still protesting feebly as they went into LaVerdiere's.

Ignoring him, Kevin went straight to the counter where Molly Durham stood. Her urge to vomit had passed off, and she felt much better. The whole thing seemed a little silly now, like a nightmare you have and then wake up from and after the initial relief you think: *I was afraid of* THAT? *How could I ever have thought* THAT *was really happening to me, even in a dream?*

But when the Delevan boy presented his drawn white face at the counter, she *knew* how you could be afraid, yes, oh yes, even of things as ridiculous as the things which happened in dreams, because she was tumbled back into her own waking dreamscape again.

The thing was, Kevin Delevan had almost the same *look* on his face: as though he were so deep inside somewhere that when his voice and his gaze finally reached her, they seemed almost expended.

"Pop Merrill was in here," he said. "What did he buy?"

"Please excuse my son," Mr. Delevan said. "He's not feeling w—"

Then *he* saw *Molly's* face and stopped. She looked like she had just seen a man lose his arm to a factory machine.

"Oh!" she said. "Oh my God!"

"Was it film?" Kevin asked her.

"What's wrong with him?" Molly asked faintly. "I *knew* something was the minute he walked in. What is it? Has he . . . done something?"

Jesus, John Delevan thought. *He* DOES *know. It's all true, then.*

169

At that moment, Mr. Delevan made a quietly heroic decision: he gave up entirely. He gave up entirely and put himself and what he believed could and could not be true entirely in his son's hands.

"It was, wasn't it?" Kevin pressed her. His urgent face rebuked her for her flutters and tremors. "Polaroid film. From *that*." He pointed at the display.

"Yes." Her complexion was as pale as china; the bit of rouge she had put on that morning stood out in hectic, flaring patches. "He was so . . . strange. Like a talking doll. What's wrong with him? What—"

But Kevin had whirled away, back to his father.

"I need a camera," he rapped. "I need it right now. A Polaroid Sun 660. They have them. They're even on special. See?"

And in spite of his decision, Mr. Delevan's mouth would not quite let go of the last clinging shreds of rationality. "Why—" he began, and that was as far as Kevin let him get.

"*I don't KNOW why!*" he shouted, and Molly Durham moaned. She didn't want to throw up now; Kevin Delevan was scary, but not *that* scary. What she wanted to do right now was simply go home and creep up to her bedroom and draw the covers over her head. "*But we have to have it, and time's almost up, Dad!*"

"Give me one of those cameras," Mr. Delevan said, drawing his wallet out with shaking hands, unaware that Kevin had already darted to the display.

"Just take one," she heard a trembling voice entirely unlike her own say. "Just take one and go."

CHAPTER NINETEEN

Across the square, Pop Merrill, who believed he was peacefully repairing a cheap cuckoo clock, innocent as a babe in arms, finished loading Kevin's camera with one of the film packs. He snapped it shut. It made its squidgy little whine.

Damn cuckoo sounds like he's got a bad case of laryngitis. Slipped a gear, I guess. Well, I got the cure for that.

"I'll fix you," Pop said, and raised the camera. He applied one blank eye to the viewfinder with the hairline crack which was so tiny you didn't even see it when you got your eye up to it. The camera was aimed at the front of the store, but *that* didn't matter; wherever you pointed it, it was aimed at a certain black dog that wasn't any dog God had ever made in a little town called for the want of a better word Polaroidsville, which He also hadn't ever made.

FLASH!

That squidgy little whine as Kevin's camera pushed out a new picture.

"There," Pop said with quiet satisfaction. "Maybe I'll do more than get you talking, bird. What I mean to say is I might just get you *singing.* I don't promise, but I'll give her a try."

Pop grinned a dry, leathery grin and pushed the button again.

FLASH!

They were halfway across the square when John Delevan saw a silent white light fill the dirty windows of the Emporium Galorium. The *light* was silent, but following it, like an aftershock, he heard a low, dark rumble that seemed to come to his

171

ears from the old man's junk-store . . . but only because the old man's junk-store was the only place it could find a way to get out. Where it seemed to be *emanating* from was under the earth . . . or was it just that the earth itself seemed the only place large enough to cradle the owner of that voice?

"Run, Dad!" Kevin cried. *"He's started doing it!"*

That flash recurred, lighting the windows like a heatless stroke of electricity. It was followed by that subaural growl again, the sound of a sonic boom in a wind-tunnel, the sound of some animal which was horrible beyond comprehension being kicked out of its sleep.

Mr. Delevan, helpless to stop himself and almost unaware of what he was doing, opened his mouth to tell his son that a light that big and bright could not possibly be coming from the built-in flash of a Polaroid camera, but Kevin had already started to run.

Mr. Delevan began to run himself, knowing perfectly well what he meant to do: catch up to his son and collar him and drag him away before something dreadful beyond his grasp of all dreadful things could happen.

CHAPTER TWENTY

The second Polaroid Pop took forced the first one out of the slot. It fluttered down to the top of the desk, where it landed with a thud heavier than such a square of chemically treated cardboard could possibly make. The Sun dog filled almost the entire frame now; the foreground was its impossible head, the black pits of the eyes, the smoking, teeth-filled jaws. The skull seemed to be elongating into a shape like a bullet or a teardrop as the dog-thing's speed and the shortening distance between it and the lens combined to drive it further out of focus. Only the tops of the pickets in the fence behind it were visible now; the bulk of the thing's flexed shoulders ate up the rest of the frame.

Kevin's birthday string tie, which had rested next to the Sun camera in his drawer, showed at the bottom of the frame, winking back a shaft of hazy sunlight.

"Almost got you, you son of a whore," Pop said in a high, cracked voice. His eyes were blinded by the light. He saw neither dog nor camera. He saw only the voiceless cuckoo which had become his life's mission. "You'll sing, damn you! I'll *make* you sing!"

FLASH!

The third picture pushed the second from the slot. It fell too fast, more like a chunk of stone than a square of cardboard, and when it hit the desk, it dug through the ancient frayed blotter there and sent startled splinters flying up from the wood beneath.

In this picture, the dog's head was torn even further out of focus; it had become a long column of flesh that gave it a strange, almost three-dimensional aspect.

In the third one, still poking out of the slot in the bottom of the camera, the Sun dog's snout seemed, impossibly, to be coming back into focus again. It was impossible because it was as close to the lens as it could get; so close it seemed to be the snout of some sea-monster just below that fragile meniscus we call the surface.

"Damn thing still ain't quite right," Pop said.

His finger pushed the Polaroid's trigger again.

CHAPTER TWENTY-ONE

Kevin ran up the steps of the Emporium Galorium. His father reached for him, caught nothing but the air an inch from the fluttering tail of Kevin's shirt, stumbled, and landed on the heels of his hands. They slid across the second step from the top, sending a quiver of small splinters into his skin.

"Kevin!"

He looked up and for a moment the world was almost lost in another of those dazzling white flashes. This time the roar was much louder. It was the sound of a crazed animal on the verge of making its weakening cage give it up. He saw Kevin with his head down, one hand shielding his eyes from the white glare, frozen in that stroboscopic light as if he himself had turned into a photograph. He saw cracks like quicksilver jig-jag their way down the show windows.

"Kevin, look ou—"

The glass burst outward in a glittery spray and Mr. Delevan ducked his own head. Glass flew around him in a squall. He felt it patter into his hair and both cheeks were scratched, but none of the glass dug deeply into either the boy or the man; most of it had been pulverized to crumbs.

There was a splintering crunch. He looked up again and saw that Kevin had gained entry just as Mr. Delevan had thought they might earlier: by ramming the now-glassless door with his shoulder and tearing the new locking bolt right through the old, rotted wood.

"KEVIN, GODDAMMIT!" he bawled. He got up, almost stumbled to one knee again as his feet tangled together, then lurched upright and plunged after his son.

• • •

Something had happened to the goddam cuckoo clock. Something *bad*.

It was striking again and again—bad enough, but that wasn't all. It had also gained weight in Pop's hands . . . and it seemed to be growing uncomfortably hot, as well.

Pop looked down at it, and suddenly tried to scream in horror through jaws which felt as if they had been wired together somehow.

He realized he had been struck blind, and he *also* suddenly realized that what he held was not a cuckoo clock at all.

He tried to make his hands relax their death-grip on the camera and was horrified to find he could not open his fingers. The field of gravity around the camera seemed to have increased. And the horrid thing was growing steadily hotter. Between Pop's splayed, white-nailed fingers, the gray plastic of the camera's housing had begun to smoke.

His right index finger began to crawl upward toward the red shutter-button like a crippled fly.

"No," he muttered, and then, in a plea: *"Please . . ."*

His finger paid no attention. It reached the red button and settled upon it just as Kevin slammed his shoulder into the door and burst in. Glass from the door's panes crunched and sprayed.

Pop didn't push the button. Even blind, even feeling the flesh of his fingers begin to smoulder and scorch, he knew he didn't push the button. But as his finger settled upon it, that gravitational field first seemed to double, then treble. He tried to hold his finger up and off the button. It was like trying to hold the push-up position on the planet Jupiter.

"Drop it!" the kid screamed from somewhere out on the rim of his darkness. "Drop it, *drop it!*"

"NO!" Pop screamed back. *"What I mean to say is I CAN'T!"*

The red button began to slide in toward its contact point.

• • •

176

Kevin was standing with his legs spread, bent over the camera they had just taken from LaVerdiere's, the box it had come in lying at his feet. He had managed to hit the button that released the front of the camera on its hinge, revealing the wide loading slot. He was trying to jam one of the film packs into it, and it stubbornly refused to go—it was as if this camera had turned traitor, too, possibly in sympathy to its brother.

Pop screamed again, but this time there were no words, only an inarticulate cry of pain and fear. Kevin smelled hot plastic and roasting flesh. He looked up and saw the Polaroid was melting, actually *melting,* in the old man's frozen hands. Its square, boxy silhouette was rearranging itself into an odd, hunched shape. Somehow the glass of both the viewfinder and the lens had also become plastic. Instead of breaking or popping out of the camera's increasingly shapeless shell, they were elongating and drooping like taffy, becoming a pair of grotesque eyes like those in a mask of tragedy.

Dark plastic, heated to a sludge like warm wax, ran over Pop's fingers and the backs of his hands in thick runnels, carving troughs in his flesh. The plastic cauterized what it burned, but Kevin saw blood squeezing from the sides of these runnels and dripping down Pop's flesh to strike the table in smoking droplets which sizzled like hot fat.

"Your film's still wrapped up!" his father bawled from behind him, breaking Kevin's paralysis. *"Unwrap it! Give it to me!"*

His father reached around him, bumping Kevin so hard he almost knocked him over. He snatched the film pack, with its heavy paper-foil wrapping still on it, and ripped the end. He stripped it off.

"HELP ME!" Pop screeched, the last coherent words either of them heard him say.

"Quick!" his father yelled, putting the fresh film pack back in his hands. "Quick!"

The sizzle of hot flesh. The patter of hot blood on the desk, what had been a shower now becoming a storm as the bigger veins and arteries in Pop's fingers and the backs of his hands began to let go. A brook of hot, running plastic braceleted his left wrist and the bundle of veins so close to the surface there let go, spraying out blood as if through a rotten gasket which has first begun to leak in several places and now begins to simply disintegrate under the insistent, beating pressure.

Pop howled like an animal.

Kevin tried to jam the film pack in again and cried out *"Fuck!"* as it still refused to go.

"It's backwards!" Mr. Delevan hollered. He tried to snatch the camera from Kevin, and Kevin tore away, leaving his father with a scrap of shirt and no more. He pulled the film pack out and for a moment it jittered on the ends of his fingers, almost dropping to the floor—which, he felt, longed to actually hump itself up into a fist and smash it when it came down.

Then he had it, turned it around, socked it home, and slammed the front of the camera, which was hanging limply downward like a creature with a broken neck, shut on its hinge.

Pop howled again, and—

FLASH!

CHAPTER TWENTY-TWO

This time it was like standing in the center of a sun which goes supernova in one sudden, heatless gust of light. Kevin felt as if his shadow had actually been hammered off his heels and driven into the wall. Perhaps this was at least partly true, for all of the wall behind him was instantly flash-baked and threaded with a thousand crazy cracks except for one sunken area where his shadow fell. His outline, as clear and unmistakable as a silhouette cut-out, was tattooed there with one elbow stuck out in a flying wedge, caught and frozen even as the arm which cast the shadow left its frozen image behind, rising to bring the new camera up to his face.

The top of the camera in Pop's hands tore free of the rest with a thick sound like a very fat man clearing his throat. The Sun dog growled, and this time that bass thunder was loud enough, clear enough, *near* enough, to shatter the glass in the fronts of the clocks and to send the glass in the mirrors and in the frames of pictures belching across the floor in momentary crystal arcs of amazing and improbable beauty.

The camera did not moan or whine this time; the sound of its mechanism was a scream, high and drilling, like a woman who is dying in the throes of a breech delivery. The square of paper which shoved and bulled its way out of that slitted opening smoked and fumed. Then the dark delivery-slot itself began to melt, one side drooping downward, the other wrinkling upward, all of it beginning to yawn like a toothless mouth. A bubble was forming upon the shiny surface of the last picture, which still hung in the widening mouth of the channel from which the Polaroid Sun gave birth to its photographs.

179

As Kevin watched, frozen, looking through a curtain of flashing, zinging dots that last white explosion had put in front of his eyes, the Sun dog roared again. The sound was smaller now, with less of that sense that it was coming from beneath and from everywhere, but it was also more deadly because it was more *real,* more *here.*

Part of the dissolving camera blew backward in a great gray gobbet, striking Pop Merrill's neck and expanding into a necklace. Suddenly both Pop's jugular vein and carotid artery gave way in spraying gouts of blood that jetted upward and outward in bright-red spirals. Pop's head whipped bonelessly backward.

The bubble on the surface of the picture grew. The picture itself began to jitter in the yawning slot at the bottom of the now-decapitated camera. Its sides began to spread, as if the picture was no longer on cardboard at all but some flexible substance like knitted nylon. It wiggled back and forth in the slot, and Kevin thought of the cowboy boots he had gotten for his birthday two years ago, and how he had had to wiggle his feet into them, because they were a little too tight.

The edges of the picture struck the edges of the camera delivery-slot, where they should have stuck firmly. But the camera was no longer a solid; was, in fact, losing all resemblance to what it had been. The edges of the picture sliced through its sides as cleanly as the razor-sharp sides of a good double-edged knife slide through tender meat. They poked through what had been the Polaroid's housing, sending gray drops of smoking plastic flying into the dim air. One landed on a dry, crumbling stack of old *Popular Mechanics* magazines and burrowed a fuming, charred hole into them.

The dog roared again, an angry, ugly sound—the cry of something with nothing but rending and killing on its mind. Those things, and nothing else.

The picture teetered on the edge of the sagging, dissolving slit, which now looked more like the bell of some misshapen wind instrument than anything else, and then fell forward to the desk with the speed of a stone tumbling into a well.

Kevin felt a hand claw at his shoulder.

"What's it doing?" his father asked hoarsely. "Jesus Christ almighty, Kevin, *what's it doing?*"

Kevin heard himself answer in a remote, almost disinterested voice: "Being born."

CHAPTER TWENTY-THREE

Pop Merrill died leaning back in the chair behind his work-table, where he had spent so many hours sitting: sitting and smoking; sitting and fixing things up so they would run for at least awhile and he could sell the worthless to the thoughtless; sitting and loaning money to the impulsive and the improvident after the sun went down. He died staring up at the ceiling, from which his own blood dripped back down to splatter on his cheeks and into his open eyes.

His chair overbalanced and spilled his lolling body onto the floor. His purse and his key-ring clattered.

On his desk, the final Polaroid continued to jiggle about restlessly. Its sides spread apart, and Kevin seemed to sense some unknown thing, both alive and not alive, groaning in horrid, unknowable labor pains.

"We've got to get out of here," his father panted, pulling at him. John Delevan's eyes were large and frenzied, riveted on that spreading, moving photograph which now covered half of Merrill's worktable. It no longer resembled a photograph at all. Its sides bulged out like the cheeks of someone trying frantically to whistle. The shiny bubble, now a foot high, humped and shuddered. Strange, unnameable colors raced aimlessly back and forth across a surface which seemed to have broken some oily sort of sweat. That roar, full of frustration and purpose and frantic hunger, ripped through his brain again and again, threatening to split it and let in madness.

Kevin pulled away from him, ripping his shirt along the shoulder. His voice was full of a deep, strange calm. "No—it would just come after us. I think it wants me, because if it wanted Pop it's already got him and I was the one who owned the camera first, anyway. But it wouldn't stop there. It'd take you, too. And it might not stop there, either."

"You can't do anything!" his father screamed.

"Yes," Kevin said. "I've got one chance."

And raised the camera.

The edges of the picture reached the edges of the worktable. Instead of lolling over, they curled up and continued to twist and spread. Now they resembled odd wings which were somehow equipped with lungs and were trying to breathe in some tortured fashion.

The entire surface of the amorphous, pulsing thing continued to puff up; what should have been flat surface had become a horrid tumor, its lumped and cratered sides trickling with vile liquid. It gave off the bland smell of head cheese.

The dog's roars had become continuous, the trapped and furious belling of a hell-hound bent on escape, and some of the late Pop Merrill's clocks began to strike again and again, as if in protest.

Mr. Delevan's frantic urge to escape had deserted him; he felt overcome by a deep and dangerous lassitude, a kind of lethal sleepiness.

Kevin held the camera's viewfinder to his eye. He had only been deer-hunting a few times, but he remembered how it was when it was your turn to wait, hidden, with your rifle as your hunting partners walked through the woods toward you, deliberately making as much noise as they could, hoping to drive something out of the trees and into the clearing where you were waiting, your field of fire a safe angle that would cross in front of the men. You didn't have to worry about hitting them; you only had to worry about hitting the deer.

There was time to wonder if you *could* hit it, when and if it showed itself. There was also time to wonder if you could bring yourself to fire at all. Time to hope that the deer would remain hypothetical, so the test did not have to be made . . . and so it had always turned out to be. The one time there *had* been a deer, his father's friend Bill Roberson had been lying up in the blind. Mr. Roberson had put the bullet just where you were supposed to put it, at the juncture of neck and shoulder, and they had gotten the game-warden to take their pictures around it, a twelve-point buck any man would be happy to brag on.

Bet you wish it'd been your turn in the puckies, don't you, son? the game-warden had asked, ruffling Kevin's hair (he had been twelve then, the growth spurt which had begun about seventeen months ago and which had so far taken him to just an inch under six feet still a year away . . . which meant he had not been big enough to be resentful of a man who wanted to ruffle his hair). Kevin had nodded, keeping his secret to himself: he was *glad* it hadn't been his turn in the puckies, his the rifle which must be responsible for throwing the slug or not throwing it . . . and, if he had turned out to have the courage to do the shooting, his reward would have been only another troublesome responsibility: to shoot the buck clean. He didn't know if he could have mustered the courage to put another bullet in the thing if the kill *wasn't* clean, or the strength to chase the trail of its blood and steaming, startled droppings and finish what he had started if it ran.

He had smiled up at the game-warden and nodded and his dad had snapped a picture of *that,* and there had never been any need to tell his dad that the thought going on behind that upturned brow and under the game-warden's ruffling hand had been *No. I don't wish it. The world is full of tests, but twelve's too young to go hunting them. I'm glad it was Mr. Roberson. I'm not ready yet to try a man's tests.*

But now he was the one in the blind, wasn't he? And the animal was coming, wasn't it? And it was no harmless eater of grasses this time, was it? This was a killing engine big enough and mean enough to swallow a tiger whole, and it meant to kill *him,* and that was only for starters, and he was the only one that could stop it.

The thought of turning the Polaroid over to his father crossed his mind, but only momentarily. Something deep inside himself knew the truth: to pass the camera would be tantamount to murdering his father and committing suicide himself. His father believed *something,* but that wasn't specific enough. The camera wouldn't work for his father even if his father managed to break out of his current stunned condition and press the shutter.

It would only work for him.

So he waited on the test, peering through the viewfinder of the camera as if it were the gunsight of a rifle, peering at the photograph as it continued to spread and force that shiny, liquescent bubble wider and wider and higher and higher.

Then the actual birthing of the Sun dog into this world began to happen. The camera seemed to gain weight and turn to lead as the thing roared again with a sound like a whiplash loaded with steel shot. The camera trembled in his hands and he could feel his wet, slippery fingers simply wanting to uncurl and let go. He held on, his lips pulling back from his teeth in a sick and desperate grin. Sweat ran into one eye, momentarily doubling his vision. He threw his head back, snapping his hair off his forehead and out of his eyebrows, and then nestled his staring eye back into the viewfinder as a great ripping sound, like heavy cloth being torn in half by strong, slow hands, filled the Emporium Galorium.

The shiny surface of the bubble tore open. Red smoke, like the blast from a tea-kettle set in front of red neon, billowed out.

The thing roared again, an angry, homicidal sound. A gigantic jaw, filled with croggled teeth, burst up through the shrivelling membrane of the now-collapsing bubble like the jaw of a breaching pilot whale. It ripped and chewed and gnawed at the membrane, which gave way with gummy splattering sounds.

The clocks struck wildly, crazily.

His father grabbed him again, so hard that Kevin's teeth rapped against the plastic body of the camera and it came within a hair of spilling out of his hands and shattering on the floor.

"*Shoot it!*" his father screamed over the thing's bellowing din. "*Shoot it, Kevin, if you can shoot it,* SHOOT IT NOW, *Christ Jesus, it's going to—*"

Kevin yanked away from his father's hand. "Not yet," he said. "Not just y—"

The thing *screamed* at the sound of Kevin's voice. The Sun dog lunged up from wherever it was, driving the picture still wider. It gave and stretched with a groaning sound. This was replaced by the thick cough of ripping fabric again.

And suddenly the Sun dog was up, its head rising black and rough and tangled through the hole in reality like some weird periscope which was all tangled metal and glittering, glaring lenses . . . except it wasn't metal but that twisted, spiky fur Kevin was looking at, and those were not lenses but the thing's insane, raging eyes.

It caught at the neck, the spines of its pelt shredding the edges of the hole it had made into a strange sunburst pattern. It roared again, and sickly yellow-red fire licked out of its mouth.

John Delevan took a step backward and struck a table overloaded with thick copies of *Weird Tales* and *Fantastic Universe.* The table tilted and Mr. Delevan flailed helplessly against it, his heels first rocking back and then shooting out from under him. Man and table went over with a crash. The Sun dog roared again, then dipped its head with an unsuspected delicacy and tore at the membrane which held it. The membrane ripped. The thing barked out a thin stream of fire which ignited the membrane and turned it to ash. The beast lunged upward again and Kevin saw that the thing on the tie around its neck was no longer a tie-clasp but the spoon-shaped tool which Pop Merrill had used to clean his pipe.

In that moment a clean calmness fell over the boy. His father bellowed in surprise and fear as he tried to untangle himself from the table he had fallen over, but Kevin took no notice. The cry seemed to come from a great distance away.

It's all right, Dad, he thought, fixing the struggling, emerging beast more firmly in the viewfinder. *It's all right, don't you see? It* can *be all right, anyway . . . because the charm it wears has changed.*

He thought that perhaps the Sun dog had its master, too . . . and its master had realized that Kevin was no longer sure prey.

And perhaps there was a dog-catcher in that strange nowhere town of Polaroidsville; there must be, else why had the fat woman been in his dream? It was the fat woman who had told him what he must do, either on her own or because that dog-catcher had put her there for him to see and notice: the two-dimensional fat woman with her two-dimensional shopping-cart full of two-dimensional cameras. *Be careful, boy. Pop's dog broke his leash and he's a mean un. . . . It's hard to take his pitcher, but you can't do it at all, 'less you have a cam'ra.*

And now he had his camera, didn't he? It was not sure, not by any means, but at least he had it.

The dog paused, head turning almost aimlessly . . . until its muddy, burning gaze settled on Kevin Delevan. Its black lips peeled back from its corkscrewed boar's fangs, its muzzle opened to reveal the smoking channel of its throat, and it gave a high, drilling howl of fury. The ancient hanging globes that lit Pop's place at night shattered one after another in rows, sending down spinning shards of frosted fly-beshitted glass. It lunged, its broad, panting chest bursting through the membrane between the worlds.

Kevin's finger settled on the Polaroid's trigger.

It lunged again, and now its front legs popped free, and those cruel spurs of bone, so like gigantic thorns, scraped and scrabbled for purchase on the desk. They dug long vertical scars in the heavy rock-maple. Kevin could hear the dusky thud-and-scratch of its pistoning rear legs digging for a grip down there (wherever *down there* was), and he knew that this was the final short stretch of seconds in which it would be trapped and at his mercy; the next convulsive lunge would send it flying over the desk, and once free of the hole through which it was squirming, it would move as fast as liquid death, charging across the space between them, setting his pants ablaze with its fiery breath split-seconds before it tore into his warm innards.

Very clearly, Kevin instructed: "Say *cheese*, you mother-fucker."

And triggered the Polaroid.

CHAPTER TWENTY-FOUR

The flash was so bright that Kevin could not conceive of it later; could, in fact, barely remember it at all. The camera he was holding did not grow hot and melt; instead there were three or four quick, decisive breaking sounds from inside it as its ground-glass lenses burst and its springs either snapped or simply disintegrated.

In the white afterglare he saw the Sun dog *frozen,* a perfect black-and-white Polaroid photograph, its head thrown back, every twisting fold and crevasse in its wildly bushed-out fur caught like the complicated topography of a dry river-valley. Its teeth shone, no longer subtly shaded yellow but as white and nasty as old bones in that sterile emptiness where water had quit running millennia ago. Its single swollen eye, robbed of the dark and bloody porthole of iris by the merciless flash, was as white as an eye in the head of a Greek bust. Smoking snot drizzled from its flared nostrils and ran like hot lava in the narrow gutters between its rolled-back muzzle and its gums.

It was like a negative of all the Polaroids Kevin had ever seen: black-and-white instead of color, and in three dimensions instead of two. And it was like watching a living creature turned instantly to stone by a careless look at the head of Medusa.

"You're *done,* you son of a bitch!" Kevin screamed in a cracked, hysterical voice, and as if in agreement, the thing's frozen forelegs lost their hold on the desk and it began to disappear, first slowly and then rapidly, into the hole from which it had come. It went with a rocky coughing sound, like a landslide.

What would I see if I ran over now and looked into that hole? he wondered incoherently. *Would I see that house, that fence, the old man with his shopping-cart, staring with wide-eyed wonder at the face of a giant, not a boy but a Boy, staring back at him from a torn and charred hole in the hazy sky? Would it suck me in? What?*

Instead, he dropped the Polaroid and raised his hands to his face.

Only John Delevan, lying on the floor, saw the final act: the twisted, dead membrane shrivelling in on itself, pulling into a complicated but unimportant node around the hole, crumpling there, and then falling (or being *inhaled*) into itself.

There was a whooping sound of air, which rose from a broad gasp to a thin tea-kettle whistle.

Then it turned inside-out and was gone. Simply gone, as if it had never been.

Getting slowly and shakily to his feet, Mr. Delevan saw that the final inrush (or outrush, he supposed, depending on which side of that hole you were on) of air had pulled the desk-blotter and the other Polaroids the old man had taken in with it.

His son was standing in the middle of the floor with his hands over his face, weeping.

"Kevin," he said quietly, and put his arms around his boy.

"I had to take its picture," Kevin said through his tears and through his hands. "It was the only way to get rid of it. I had to take the rotten whoredog's picture. *That's* what I mean to say."

"Yes." He hugged him tighter. "Yes, and you did it."

Kevin looked at his father with naked, streaming eyes. *"That's* how I had to shoot it, Dad. Do you see?"

"Yes," his father said. "Yes, I see that." He kissed Kevin's hot cheek again. "Let's go home, son."

He tightened his grip around Kevin's shoulders, wanting to lead him toward the door and away from the smoking, bloody body of the old man (Kevin hadn't really noticed yet, Mr. Delevan thought, but if they spent much longer here, he would), and for a moment Kevin resisted him.

"What are people going to *say?*" Kevin asked, and his tone was so prim and spinsterish that Mr. Delevan laughed in spite of his own sizzling nerves.

"Let them say whatever they want," he told Kevin. "They'll never get within shouting distance of the truth, and I don't think anyone will try very hard, anyway." He paused. "No one really liked him much, you know."

"I never *want* to be in shouting distance of the truth," Kevin whispered. "Let's go home."

"Yes. I love you, Kevin."

"I love you, too," Kevin said hoarsely, and they went out of the smoke and the stink of old things best left forgotten and into the bright light of day. Behind them, a pile of old magazines burst into flame . . . and the fire was quick to stretch out its hungry orange fingers.

EPILOGUE

It was Kevin Delevan's sixteenth birthday, and he got exactly what he wanted: a WordStar 70 PC and word processor. It was a seventeen-hundred-dollar toy, and his parents could never have afforded it in the old days, but in January, about three months after that final confrontation in the Emporium Galorium, Aunt Hilda had died quietly in her sleep. She had indeed Done Something for Kevin and Meg; had, in fact, Done Quite a Lot for the Whole Family. When the will cleared probate in early June, the Delevans found themselves richer by nearly seventy thousand dollars . . . and that was after taxes, not before.

"Jeez, it's neat! Thank you!" Kevin cried, and kissed his mother, his father, and even his sister, Meg (who giggled but, being a year older, made no attempt to rub it off; Kevin couldn't decide if this change was a step in the right direction or not). He spent much of the afternoon in his room, fussing over it and trying out the test program.

Around four o'clock, he came downstairs and into his father's den. "Where's Mom and Meg?" he asked.

"They've gone out to the crafts fair at . . . Kevin? Kevin, what's wrong?"

"You better come upstairs," Kevin said hollowly.

At the door to his room, he turned his pale face toward his father's equally pale face. There was something more to pay, Mr. Delevan had been thinking as he followed his son up the stairs. Of course there was. And hadn't he also learned that from Reginald Marion "Pop" Merrill? The debt you incurred was what hurt you.

It was the *interest* that broke your back.

"Can we get another one of these?" Kevin asked, pointing to the laptop computer which stood open on his desk, glowing a mystic yellow oblong of light onto the blotter.

"I don't know," Mr. Delevan said, approaching the desk. Kevin stood behind him, a pallid watcher. "I guess, if we *had* to—"

He stopped, looking down at the screen.

"I booted up the word-processing program and typed 'The quick brown fox jumped over the lazy sleeping dog,'" Kevin said. "Only *that* was what came out of the printer."

Mr. Delevan stood, silently reading the hard copy. His hands and forehead felt very cold. The words there read:

> The dog is loose again.
> It is not sleeping.
> It is not lazy.
> It's coming for you, Kevin.

The original debt was what hurt you, he thought again; it was the interest that broke your back. The last two lines read:

> It's very hungry.
> And it's VERY angry.